# EMBERS OF HOPE

AF658052

# EMBERS OF HOPE

## A Journey to Light the Dark

AASHVI SINGH

LAUNCHPAD

An imprint of
Srishti Publishers & Distributors

**Srishti Publishers & Distributors**
A unit of AJR Publishing LLP
212A, Peacock Lane
Shahpur Jat, New Delhi – 110 049

editorial@srishtipublishers.com

First Published by Launchpad,
an imprint of Srishti Publishers & Distributors in 2025

Copyright © Aashvi Singh, 2025

10 9 8 7 6 5 4 3 2 1

This is a work of fiction. The characters, places, organizations and events described in this book are either a work of the author's imagination or have been used fictitiously. Any resemblance to people, living or dead, places, events, communities or organizations is purely coincidental.

The author asserts the moral right to be identified as the author of this work.

All rights reserved. No part of this publication may be reproduced, stored in a retrieval system, or transmitted, in any form or by any means, electronic, mechanical, photocopying, recording or otherwise, without the prior written permission of the Publishers.

*A wild adventure told*
*by a gifted young storyteller.*

—Ciara Geraghty

*This book is dedicated to my wonderful family.*

*To my grandparents, whose stories were the first spark of my imagination,*

*To my parents, whose love and encouragement have always been my guiding light,*

*To my uncle and aunt, who taught me to dream beyond the stars,*

*To my younger brother, my lifelong partner in adventures big and small,*

*And to my cousins, who made every ordinary day extraordinary.*

*This tale of bravery, magic, and boundless wonder is for all of you—*

*The ones who make life its own unforgettable adventure.*

# Introduction

I am the storyweaver who has spun this tale from the threads of magic and time. I bear dark, black, colossal wings that carry me through the realms of stories and time. My eyes can delve into the depths of people's souls; my ears can capture the whispers of their deepest longings. Behold my cape of stars and moons! How it glimmers and gleams. How it enchants.

Cling to my back and soar with me, reader, as we traverse black holes, traverse dazzling galaxies, and traverse endless space, pausing at a little blue-and-green planet called earth. This story is ancient, and I know the earth you inhabit has lost much of its magic.

Or has it?

Yes, the tale I am guiding you through is brimming with magic, and perhaps the earth that is your home has yet to relinquish all its enchantment. Our story commences in a humble village on the surface of this life-sustaining planet, where two exceptional twins, Annie and Jack, reside. Annie, with her fiery spirit and unwavering resolve, and Jack, with his serene and analytical mind, are not just ordinary children. Yet, this is where the narrative takes a turn. For someone is scheming in her fortress, determined to exact revenge. Will these twins, with their unique powers and unbreakable bond, be able to safeguard the world? Or will they condemn the world to the witch? Will they emerge unharmed? Or will they have to make sacrifices?

# 1.
# A VILLAGE VEILED IN MYSTERY

Long before maps were drawn and kingdoms rose from the dust, there existed a place whispered of only in ancient tales—untouched by time and cloaked in secrecy. This was Elysium, a hidden continent where the impossible was ordinary, and magic flowed like the wind, invisible yet everywhere.

The air in Elysium was alive, shimmering with enchantment. Its landscapes were otherworldly: rolling hills carpeted with flowers that glowed faintly in the moonlight, forests so dense and ancient that even the sunlight seemed hesitant to disturb them, and lakes that held secrets beneath their crimson, blood-like surface.

Legends spoke of the lakes—if you dared to swim in them, your skin would emerge stained the colour of blood, a mark that would never fade. The rivers, winding like silver serpents, were home to water dragons with shimmering scales that refracted sunlight like rainbows. These dragons were fierce but wise, and it was said they would grant passage to only the bravest souls. There were not ordinary magicians living in Elysium; they were Elemental Shifters, beings who could command the very fabric of nature. At will, they could become birds soaring through the skies, beasts prowling the forests, or even embodiments of fire, water, wind, or earth.

Elysium's magic wasn't merely an ability—it was life itself. It pulsed in the rivers, whispered in the winds, and sparked in the tiniest blades of grass. Yet, despite its breathtaking beauty, Elysium was not a land of peace. Magic, as powerful as it was, came with its dangers.

For centuries, the people of Elysium lived in harmony, guided by the Elemental Shifters. But now, whispers carried on the wind spoke of unrest. The magic of Elysium was faltering, behaving unpredictably. The lakes began to boil, the rivers overflowed with anger, and the skies grew darker each night. Some said the balance had been disturbed; others spoke of a powerful force awakening deep within the earth, a force older than the magic itself.

Whatever the reason, it left a deepening impact on Elysium. The lakes and rivers began to dry up, leaving no home for the aquatic creatures. The forests shrivelled, leaving no home for the woodland creatures. The sun beat down mercilessly. The magic of Elysium died out, and the Elemental Shifters died with it.

In the heart of this magical land stood the source of Elysium's power. Elysium's power came from a village in the centre of Elysium. This was a secret village called Sleepyfield, hidden from the rest of Elysium by a magical mist. A vast forest of tall trees surrounded this village; their tops were always covered in snow, even in the summer! Sleepyfield was where anything seemed possible when life was normal, but when Elysium's magic died, Sleepyfield's magic died too. The villagers living in Sleepyfield had a tough time fulfilling their daily needs. They had trouble finding food, and their traps never seemed to catch anything. It took them weeks—sometimes an eternity—to wait for their food to grow. Nonetheless, Sleepyfield persevered and left a resilient heritage ingrained in its past.

The grown-ups didn't have much food, so they gave the kids and the older people whatever was left. They stayed hungry, and after a while, they became fragile, like skeletons, so weak they could barely move. Water was a whole different problem. They waited for rain, then caught the water in these big iron and clay pots. To ensure the water was safe, they hung the pots on sticks and placed them over a fire, burning away all the impurities. Once the water was heated, they stored it in clay pots for later use. It was tough, but that's how they made it through.

Around this time, a powerful sorcerer and his sister lived in Asia. One day, they heard about the village of Sleepyfield, where people were struggling to make a living. Curious and wanting to help, they decided to visit. They discovered Elysium when its magic died, making it vulnerable to the rest of the world.

When they arrived, the villagers greeted them kindly, though the children gave them curious looks. The villagers, wearing tattered brown clothes, appeared weak, thin, and dishevelled. But the sorcerer was tall, strong, and wise. He was dressed in a purple velvet robe with shiny silver stars sewn into it and a matching hat. His face was kind, and his long brown hair and beard flowed to his waist.

His sister looked a lot like him but was much younger. She did not have a beard, though. She wore beautiful makeup on her friendly face and had old bracelets from when she was a baby, back when the sorcerer first learned magic. She, too, wore a fancy black robe with silver stars.

Even though the villagers didn't have much, they still treated the sorcerer and his sister with respect, giving them the best food and clean water they had. One day, some villagers walked in on the sorcerer while he was practising magic. Amazed, they asked if he could help with their problems. The sorcerer agreed, offering to enchant the forest and the village so the people would always have everything they needed. But first, he asked them to gather everyone in the village square.

Everyone in the village, kids, grown-ups, grandparents, and even teenagers, gathered in the middle of the town, all curious to see what would happen next. The tall, wise sorcerer looked around at them and said, "I'm going to enchant your village to help you all. Are you ready?"

The villagers were at a loss for words at first. They whispered to each other, unsure of what was about to happen. After a few minutes, they agreed to let the sorcerer use his magic.

The sorcerer smiled and said, "All right then. But please step back and stand far from me for your safety."

Everyone quickly shuffled back, hearts racing excitedly, wondering what fantastic magic they would witness!

The villagers took a few steps back but could still see everything. The sorcerer waved his hands, and suddenly, waves of hot, black light flowed from his fingers as he chanted in a language no one understood. The words sounded ancient, as if they hadn't been spoken in centuries.

Suddenly, with a powerful motion, he placed his hands on the ground. Immediately, the sky turned a vibrant blue, the tops of the trees turned a bright and dazzling emerald green, the tree trunks shifted to every shade of brown, and among the grass, flowers grew, covering the land in colour. It was like Sleepyfield had been dipped in a rainbow of vibrant colours.

The dark, cold caves where the villagers had lived after the magic died out transformed into cosy little cottages, and their torn, old rags became soft, comfortable clothes just right for the season.

The sorcerer declared, "You have to hold the soil in your hand and ask for whatever you want, and you will have it." The people stared at the sorcerer in shock as their village transformed into a vibrant, fantastic environment.

Sleepyfield had become a cheerful, bright place full of life. The cottages were strong, sturdy, and beautiful, like little homes from a storybook. The villagers were happy because now they had everything they could wish for.

The villagers gathered at the village square, exchanging laughter and sharing everyday stories. Everyone was happy, and the kids were no longer hungry. It seemed as though the village had finally reached its ideal state of happiness and goodwill, a place where people could live in harmony.

The villagers didn't know any magic, so the sorcerer decided to help by starting a magic school for the kids! They learned all kinds of cool beginner spells at the school—nothing too hard, just stuff anyone could do. There were spells to help you find your way home if you got lost, spells to make chores easier (like cleaning your room or washing dishes), and even spells to fix things when they broke, like toys or tools.

The kids were super excited because "Spells" was just one of the four subjects they could learn at the school! Hexes, Jinxes, and Potions classes were also for older kids and adults. It seemed like the most enjoyable school ever!

Spells were used almost every day in the village! You could use them for defence, attacks, and everyday stuff, like knitting a sweater for your kid while you wash the dishes. Everyone knew basic spells.

Curses? Those were for lawbreakers. If someone did something terrible, a curse was the way to stop them. Curses were tough to break and could be painful, so people feared them.

Hexes were like baby curses—they didn't last forever. You'd only use them to teach someone a lesson, like a quick timeout for bad behaviour.

Jinxes were all about bad luck! You'd cast a jinx if you wanted to mess with someone's day or give them a little mischief.

Potions were the next most helpful thing after spells. You could do anything with potions! Make people tell the truth, play funny pranks, solve big problems, or even mesmerize someone. There was a potion for everything you could think of! Only the village elders knew all the powerful potions, however. The villagers stuck to easy ones like curing fever or helping with minor aches and pains.

Sleepyfield was perfect. Well, except for two enigmatic figures, Wanda and the sorcerer's sister. They became close friends when the sorcerer's sister stumbled upon her in the forest outside Sleepyfield. She was about the same age, but she looked awful—her clothes were all torn, and she was covered in cuts and bruises. She sat under a tree, crying so hard that she didn't even notice anyone was there. The sorcerer's sister came closer and gently asked, "Who are you? What are you doing here? Do you live around here?"

"I'm Wanda," she whispered, her voice shaky. "I don't live here. Bandits attacked us... my parents and me. We were travelling when they came out of nowhere. I ran as fast as I could, but I could still hear my parents screaming... as they..." She trailed off, wiping away her tears.

"I've been lost ever since."

"Oh, you poor thing," she said softly, her heart breaking for Wanda. "I'll take care of you now. You won't ever have to go through something that terrible again. I promise."

So, the sorcerer's sister took Wanda in, and they remained inseparable ever since. By the time Wanda had brainwashed the sorcerer's sister, the sorcerer had married the daughter of a friendly villager and became the father of two lovely kids: a one-year-old girl and a newborn boy. One night, curious about how his sister's new friend was doing, the sorcerer wandered over to check on them. But when he got close, he heard... evil giggles. He hid behind a rock and watched. Black mist swirled around the hands of his sister and Wanda, filled with horrible images—screaming children, monsters, and torture. They began looking younger, and the spots on their hands amazingly vanished. Unbelievable as it seemed, they were becoming younger right before his eyes. Unable to hide any longer, the sorcerer stepped out, his voice filled with disbelief. "What are you up to?" he demanded.

"N-n-nothing," Wanda and the sorcerer's sister said simultaneously, their voices shaky and nervous.

But the sorcerer wasn't fooled. He looked at them with a serious, almost scary, expression and said, "No, you are not doing anything. I saw everything."

Wanda and his sister stood frozen, not knowing what to say.

"Before I punish you," the sorcerer continued, "you must leave this place before dawn. I don't want the villagers to discover that my sister has been messing with such unholy magic."

The air felt heavy, and Wanda and the sister knew he wasn't kidding. They'd have to go, and fast.

They travelled far, leaving traps and obstacles behind them, and built a vast, dark castle far away from Sleepyfield. The sorcerer did his best to protect the village, casting spells to keep it safe, but his heart wasn't in it. He was still so sad about banishing his sister for practising dark magic. His grief made his spells weaker than usual.

His sister and Wanda repeatedly tried to attack the village and get revenge, but they failed every time. That is, until one night, three years later. That night, they finally broke through. Deep in sleep, the sorcerer was suddenly awakened by loud noises. Jumping out of bed, he ran outside, only to see his sister and Wanda destroying everything and casting dark magic around the village. His worst fear had come true.

A huge battle broke out in Sleepyfield, shaking the village for an entire day! The sorcerer was mighty, and he wasn't going down quickly. He deflected every spell Wanda and the sorcerer's sister threw at him like it was nothing. And his counter-attacks? Way stronger, blasting back with even more force!

But Wanda had a secret plan. The sorcerer's sister had whispered to her during the fight, telling her to steal an ancient book called Iterus. It was no ordinary book—it held most of the sorcerer's magic, passed down through his family for generations. Wanda snuck away, found Iterus, and took it. As soon as the sorcerer realized what had happened, his strength drained away. Without Iterus, he was weak, his powers fading fast.

Standing there, weakened, the sorcerer looked at his sister and Wanda. They thought they had him cornered. But then, an idea hit him—one that could save the village forever. He thought, *If I sacrifice myself, I can enchant Sleepyfield so my sister and Wanda can never enter again. I'll even use my mind control to write in Iterus how the villagers can re-enchant the village and defeat my sister and Wanda if they ever try to attack.*

He knew his life was less important than protecting everyone in Sleepyfield, and if the villagers could gain the power of magic, they'd be able to defend themselves, too.

And so, the sorcerer contemplated how to defeat his sister and Wanda and restore the village's enchantment, his thoughts materializing in his book; he could not defeat them as he was too weak. Then, he conjured a silver knife and uttered, 'Farewell, sister!'

Before his sister or Wanda could react, he drew a deep breath, inhaled the spell required, exhaled it, plunged the knife into his heart, and lay down to rest for the final time. In an instant, a dense fog enveloped the sorcerer's sister and Wanda. When the mist dispersed, they found themselves isolated in their castle: any endeavours to breach Sleepyfield after the sorcerer's sacrifice were thwarted as the sacrifice made a protective shield around the village.

Right after the sorcerer's brave sacrifice, the villagers knew they had to do things differently to protect their village and never repeat past mistakes. So, they came together and chose five wise men, each with strong magical skills, to be the village elders. These elders were responsible for maintaining law and order in Sleepyfield.

One of these men stood out above the rest. He was super wise, like the kind of person who always knew what to do. Because of this, the villagers chose him to be the head of the elders—the leader who would make the final decisions for everyone.

Sleepyfield entered a new era of hope and promise with this new group in charge. The village was safer, happier, and stronger, all thanks to the sorcerer's sacrifice. His bravery ensured that Sleepyfield would stay safe and prosperous for many generations! The villagers decided to call their new leader the "village head" because he decided what was good or bad for the village. He always knew what the right thing to do was!

The village elders all lived in houses right next to each other, with the village head's house in the middle, the biggest. Their houses were painted in every colour you could think of! There was sunset red, navy blue, deep maroon, and even bright fluorescent yellow! Each house had a front porch with weird, magical plants that the elders used to make potions. The houses were arranged in a circle, and every house had a back porch. This meant that the circle of houses was divided into fits. I mean, fifths. They could discuss any concerns they needed to consider before presenting the idea at the monthly village meeting. In the village meeting, the adults could share ideas, ask for suggestions, or answer any questions. Children were also allowed to participate in these meetings because the elders often said that children have more imagination than adults, which is indeed true.

On the village elders' doors, there were plaques, and they said, "IMPORTANT VISITS ONLY" because the elders were always super busy making potions and fixing village problems. They didn't have time for random visitors—they were too important!

The village elders all looked the same. They were Hubert, Roland, Douglas, and Silas. Hubert was chubby, Roland was short, Douglas was skinny, and Silas was tall. But with their grey hair, big bushy beards, and matching green robes, it was easy to mix them up! The only way to tell them apart was by the letters engraved on their robes—each had their initials.

The village head was different. He had a snow-white beard and moustache and wore fancy red and gold robes. His robe said "VILLAGE HEAD" in big letters, so everyone immediately knew who he was!

In the middle of the village was a special place for meetings. It had four tall pillars, a cone-shaped roof made of thatch and straw, and four chairs for the elders. But the most fantastic thing? There was a giant golden throne for the village head, sitting high above the others. The throne was covered in precious jewels, and right next to it was his golden sceptre. The sceptre had a shiny, ball-shaped top with the biggest ruby Sleepyfield had ever seen!

The village head's fancy robes and impressive throne showed his importance and influence. He was responsible for ensuring everything in Sleepyfield ran smoothly, and everyone respected him for it, even though he didn't want any respect.

The villagers had chosen the village elders and headman because they knew powerful magic that could punish lawbreakers.

The village head, along with Hubert, Roland, Douglas, and Silas, gathered everyone in the village square. The village head said, "If the sorcerer's evil sister ever attacks our village and manages to win, she'll take away our special wishing enchantment! But don't worry—with the help of the enchanted book, I can give you something even better: never-ending money!"

He told them to line up one person from each family and promised to give each of them a chest. Inside every chest, there would be a pouch with never-ending money! He said, "After I give you the chest, run to Lordia, the blacksmith, and get keys made for your chest. Keep the money safe because if the sorcerer's sister takes our wishing enchantment, we'll need it to keep the village going until we can re-enchant it!"

The villagers were amazed, knowing that with the never-ending money, they could survive even if the magic was taken away! Someone from each family lined up one by one, and the village head handed them a chest, just like he promised. Then, everyone rushed to Lordia, the blacksmith, to get their keys made. They followed his instructions perfectly.

A few months later, something strange started to happen on what seemed like a regular day. The sky turned grey, slowly at first. People didn't worry much—they didn't even open their umbrellas because it constantly drizzled, but it never rained heavily in Sleepyfield. However, that drizzle turned into heavy rain, and the rain continued to intensify.

Then, out of nowhere—BOOM! There was lightning and thunder everywhere. Suddenly, the rain was pouring so hard it felt like the clouds were dumping buckets of water on the village! It was pure chaos. Pets were whimpering, people were running around, and those standing near their doors frantically used magic to scoop water out of their houses. One house had its chimney struck by lightning, and another had its door blown off the hinges!

People who were safe inside their homes peeked out their windows and gasped in astonishment. The water was rising fast, pooling around their homes. They couldn't leave. THEY WERE TRAPPED BY A FLOOD!

# 2. PREPARING FOR THE UNKNOWN

After a few hours, the floodwater finally drained away into the sewers. But that wasn't the worst part. The water had already flooded into everyone's houses and soaked through their chests, even the village head's chest—the one that held Iterus, the sorcerer's family heirloom. And just like that, the flood had taken all their never-ending money and Iterus into the sewers.

Once the water was gone, Lordia, the blacksmith, went to the sewer with his trusty hook, hoping to fish out the lost treasure. But as he walked, he stepped on a stone, lost his balance, and slipped! In a panic, he shot a beam of magic from his hand to stop himself from falling. But it MISFIRED! Instead of saving him, the magic hit a super heavy rock, which flipped through the air and landed right on top of the entrance to the sewer!

The whole village came together, trying to use their magic to lift the rock. But their magic had grown too weak. Even when a few strong men stepped forward and finally managed to lift it, everyone watched helplessly as their money drifted farther and farther down the sewer.

The villagers were so shocked that they accidentally let go of the stone, which fell into the sewer with a giant SPLASH! All the villagers were at once drenched, and for those who had been out and about during the storm, it was a double drenching. Everyone stood there, unsure of what to do next. The sadness and disappointment on their faces were extremely high. Children and mothers had broken into sobs, with the fathers comforting them, yet nobody knew what to do. Then, Lordia, the old blacksmith with salt-and-pepper hair, wrinkled face, and bushy beard, stepped forward with a twinkle in his eye. Lordia was a trustworthy person in Sleepyfield, and when he spoke, people listened to him. He said, "We have lost our enchantment, all our money and the ancient book! Sure, the money is never-ending, but it's floating away. But don't worry—I have an idea! And it's not just any idea, it's extraordinarily brilliant! You might even call me the Village Genius after this!"

The villagers looked at him with wide eyes, waiting for his plan.

"We're going to search for treasure!" Lordia announced, smiling proudly.

Everybody was shocked by this idea. People started whispering to one another, asking if they would like to leave their homes for the village's benefit. One person would say to the person beside him, "You have to go."

And the other person would say, "No, I won't go on such a dangerous journey."

The first person would then reply, "You have to go. It is your duty."

That is how the fighting started. Nobody wanted to risk their lives, but everybody desired the treasure.

Tiny arguments about who should go to search for the treasure bubbled into hot, erupting volcanoes! People were yelling, pointing, and even pushing each other. People's noses were broken, and the village police, who were trying to keep everyone calm, rushed in and started separating the people who were arguing. No one expected the treasure hunt to cause so much havoc. Everybody was unsure if this treasure hunt could even be arranged!

And if you're wondering, "Why don't the villagers just wish for food or something to fix all this?" Well, they couldn't anymore! Even though the witch couldn't get into Sleepyfield herself, the witch had found a sneaky way to send her magic in. Her evil forces had broken the village's enchantment and stolen their never-ending money! So, the villagers were left without their magical way of getting what they needed.

But the treasure everyone talked about wasn't just any ordinary treasure. It wasn't just gold and jewels. This treasure was unique because it had a spell on it. If you said a secret code to the chest when you opened it, the treasure would never run out! And there was more: precious gems, shiny jewellery, and even treasure for the mind—like books, a rare copy of *The Story of Imsoine, Holy Daughter of God: Illustrated* and scrolls filled with wise affirmations.

So, it wasn't just about riches. The villagers were drawn to the treasure because it promised material wealth and wisdom for anyone who found it. But still, the question remained: who would be brave enough to pursue it?

The sorcerer's sister was the one guarding the treasure! She was incredibly powerful and terrifying. However, despite everyone knowing how dangerous she was, their greed overcame them. They wanted that treasure so badly that they were willing to risk anything.

You're probably wondering, "Where did the sorcerer's sister even get all that treasure?" Seven years ago, the village head and a few of his bravest friends battled the sorcerer's sister. She had started causing trouble in Sleepyfield again, messing with magic and making things go wrong. So, they had to stop her! It was a big, fierce fight, and during all the chaos, the sorcerer's sister managed to steal everything that made up the treasure! She snuck away with piles of gold, shiny jewels, and magical objects of high use.

But even though the village head and his friends were super tired from the battle, they didn't give up. They fought hard and managed to win Iterus back, the influential book the sorcerer had left behind. The sorcerer's sister may have taken the treasure, but at least they got Iterus back—though she still holds onto all that treasure to this day! And that's why everyone is so desperate to get it now.

Then, when the arguing was getting out of control, the village head stepped in. His snow-white beard and moustache made him look like a wise old wizard. When he spoke, everyone listened because his voice was full of authority and wisdom.

He said, "Lordia is right!" Everyone gasped. "And I feel that the treasure he's talking about now has something extra in it. I believe our lost money and the ancient book—the one the sorcerer used long ago to enchant our village—have been washed into that treasure!"

The villagers were stunned. Could it be true? Their missing treasure and the influential book, all in one place? The village head's words gave them hope and made them more determined than ever to get that treasure back!

"So, if we somehow retrieve the treasure, we'll have not just the treasure but also our magical book!" The village head's eyes sparkled with excitement. "All we need to do is ask. So, who would like to go to save their village and be a saviour? Who would like to go search for treasure for the benefit of their village?"

Then, two small, nervous hands shot up into the air. It was Annie and Jack, the only twins in the village. They were born at the same time—October 1st, at noon—and were turning nine years old that year. They looked so much alike that sometimes people got confused, but there was one way to tell them apart: their hair. Jack had a messy, short brown fringe that resembled little lightning bolts zigzagging across his forehead, and he always wore pants and a T-shirt. Annie also wore pants and a T-shirt, but she braided her hair into neat plaits on each side of her head.

Both were chubby with round faces, yet had distinctive cheekbones that made them stand out. Their legs were thin but strong—they had the hearts of adventurers! They had tiny, snub noses, but the most striking thing about them was their eyes. Their left eyes were blue like a clear summer sky, and their right eyes were a bright, golden yellow, just like a cat's.

Annie and Jack daydreamed about going on adventures every single day. Whenever they had free time, they would pretend to be on wild journeys, fighting dragons, meeting fire nymphs, and riding glitter-trail-leaving, shimmering unicorns. Their pet frog, Croaky, joined in every time. Croaky had orange spots on his back and bright red forearms and hind legs, and he hopped along with them wherever they went like he was part of the team.

But when the twins volunteered for the treasure hunt, the village elders—Hubert, Roland, Douglas, and Silas—looked at each other with worried faces. They were old and wise, knowing how dangerous the journey could be. "You're too young, and the dangers along the way are at their zenith. We can not allow you to go, but the village head's decision will be final," said Hubert, his voice full of concern. Roland, Douglas and Silas nodded in agreement.

Annie and Jack's hearts pounded in their chests.

Annie said determinedly, "Well, we say we are going!" Her voice was a little shaky but full of bravery. Jack is good at building things. He's like a constructor genius! And I'm great at reading maps and finding the way. We'll take all the stuff we need, like food and water, and even Croaky can come to help."

Jack nodded quickly, backing her up. "Yeah! We eat, dream and breathe such adventures, and we have upskilled our magical abilities to the next level!" he grinned.

The village head, who was old and wise with his long white beard, scratched his chin and thought deeply. We have to act fast, he worried; the sorcerer's sister and her ally are getting stronger, and our magic shield is weakening. Finally, he lifted his head, and his serious voice attracted everyone's attention.

"You may go," he said, "but beware, many dangers will await you. Sometimes it feels like you can't win, but in those moments, remember: your whole village is counting on you." He paused and looked at the twins with kind, yet serious, eyes. "I will give you the map for your journey. Be ready to leave at dawn. I trust you two because you think fast, can protect yourselves, and are smart enough to face what's coming. This mission is dangerous, but I have faith in you."

Annie and Jack nodded, their hearts pounding with excitement.

The village head led Annie and Jack to his huge house. On the way, he bent down, grabbed some soil, and squeezed it into a ball while muttering some strange words. They walked up to the front door with a shiny, jewelled knocker and a plaque that read: VILLAGE HEAD'S HOUSE—IMPORTANT VISITS ONLY.

He unlocked the door and beckoned them inside. As soon as Annie and Jack stepped in, they froze with awe. The floor featured the most beautiful marble panelling, while the ceiling boasted gold pillars with intricate carvings that supported it. The walls were adorned with portraits of the old village heads, accompanied by small pictures of their accomplishments painted around their faces.

They saw a picture of the village head on the last wall, the one standing right beside them! Feeling super curious, Annie asked, "Um, excuse me, but... where are we going?"

"To my private study," the village head said with a mysterious smile. "I have something in there that will be very useful for your journey, and I've decided to give it to you."

Jack, always curious, asked, "But... what exactly is it?"

"You'll see," the village head replied, his voice full of mystery.

He led them up to his private study. When they walked in, their eyes went wide. All four walls were covered with bookshelves except for two patches on one wall. The village head's desk sat in front of a big window, and on it was a total heap of scrolls and parchment. They were scattered across the desk.

One of the bare parts of the wall contained a strange three-legged stand. Sitting atop it was a giant gold cauldron, shimmering in the sunlight that streamed through the window.

Next to the giant cauldron was a side table heaving with spell books. The village head walked over to the second piece of wall without bookshelves and tapped it three times.

Suddenly, a secret shelf spun out from the wall! It fit perfectly into the hidden space, and an incredibly fancy, deep-blue box was on that shelf. The box was covered in shiny jewels—rubies, emeralds, diamonds, and topaz in yellow and blue. The village head opened it up, and inside was... just an old, blank sheet of parchment.

But as soon as the parchment felt the touch of the village's head's hands, something magical happened. The blank sheet instantly transformed into an intricate map, complete with small drawings and lines that showed minute curves and bends.

The village head handed it to Annie, placing it gently in her hands. "This is yours now," he said. "It will guide you through the challenges and lead you to your destination, especially if you get lost."

Then, he took the ball of soil he'd enchanted earlier and said, "This soil is now wish-soil. If you need something on your journey, ask for it, and it will be provided. You should also pack a few knives, three gas-filter handkerchiefs—which I'll give you—a big rope, some blankets, a fleece-lined sleeping bag, and some never-ending food."

Annie and Jack said together, "Thank you, village head. We'll use the map and wish-soil wisely!"

But Jack, always curious, couldn't help but ask, his voice a little shaky with excitement, "But, village head, what kind of mysteries are waiting for us? Have you ever visited the sorcerer's sister's castle to find the treasure? And... if you can enchant a ball with the same magic we had before the storm, why can't you enchant the whole village again?" The village head paused, his wise old eyes twinkling for a moment.

"Jack!" Annie whispered fiercely, glaring at him. Her brother couldn't help himself. He always asked too many questions at once, like he was trying to solve a puzzle before even starting it.

The village head chuckled softly at their little squabble, then leaned in and said, "I have been to the sorcerer's sister's castle before. However, I won't tell you what happens there. You'll find out when the time is right." He paused, his face growing serious. "I went there to find a treasure of my own once. But the sorcerer's sister, she's clever. She knew I was coming, and before I got there... she hid the treasure."

Annie and Jack's eyes grew wide as they imagined the tricky sorcerer's sister, always one step ahead.

The village head sighed deeply. "Maybe you two can find the treasure for me," he said with a bit of hope. "As for why I can't enchant the whole village again if I try, the sorcerer's sister will know. She'll take the enchantment away as soon as I do it, and then I'll do it again, and she'll retake it. It would just keep going forever! I need the ancient book to strengthen the enchantment enough to stay for good."

Annie looked up at the village head with a cheeky grin and asked, "Can we take some chocolate cosmos perfume?"

The village head raised an eyebrow, "Chocolate cosmos perfume? Why on earth would you need that?"

Annie giggled, "It's my personal favourite! Smells so good!"

The village head sighed, but a small smile tugged at his lips. "All right, all right. Wait here."

Looking back at Annie and Jack, he left the room, clearly puzzled. They looked at each other, a confused expression on their faces. After a moment, the village head returned, holding three glowing handkerchiefs.

"These," he said, holding them up, "are enchanted to help you breathe underwater and even in poisonous gas. Way more useful than perfume, right?"

Annie smirked, "I mean, the perfume could still be used at some point."

After the village head gave Jack and Annie the map and those super cool gas-filter handkerchiefs, they rushed home to pack. They stuffed their bags with everything they thought they'd need—blankets, snacks, the enchanted soil ball, and Croaky, their pet frog, hopped beside them. They were all set to leave at first light.

The following day, the entire village gathered at the gate, their faces sad and worried, as if it might be the last time they'd ever see the twins. People waved and shouted, "Good luck!" Some even cried. Annie and Jack waved back, feeling a mix of excitement and nervousness bubbling in their stomachs.

But as they disappeared down the road, something sneaky was happening behind them. A descendant of the sorcerer, up to no good, turned into... Croaky! Yep, their very own frog! He had put on a disguise so he could follow them. His plan? To put the whole village and everything around it into a deep sleep.

# 3.
# CLIMB UP THE VIOLET VULTURES

The trio—Annie, Jack, and Croaky—had been walking for what felt like forever, crossing fields, valleys, and rivers, when they finally reached a wide-open field. Ahead of them were the scariest, creepiest mountains in the world: the Violet Vultures. Everything was violet. The mountains, the few spiky trees, even the cacti, and above them, giant violet vultures flew in circles, screeching in a way that made your spine shiver.

The mountains were super steep; if you took even one wrong step, you'd slip and tumble down to your doom. And the vultures? They'd swoop in, gobbling you up faster than you could scream. Bones were scattered all over the mountains from people who tried to cross and failed. Violet flowers grew there, too, but they weren't just pretty; they were also extremely dangerous. One sniff and you'd forget everything and wander, forever lost. Too much sniffing? Your game was over.

Surrounding the mountains was a vast lake, but it wasn't just any lake. Sharp, claw-like rocks jutted up from the water like deadly fangs, forming what people called the "Devil's Teeth." Those rocks would finish you even if you survived falling off the mountain. The first person to ever see the Violet Vultures came up with a creepy saying to warn others: "If not die by the mountain, then die by rock." Annie and Jack knew this wouldn't be easy, but they had no choice—they had to cross.

Annie and Jack took a few deep breaths and stepped forward, staring up at the looming Violet Vultures. Their eyes widened as they realized the mountains had somehow closed around them when they weren't looking, almost trapping them, except for where they had come from. Annie's voice was shaky as she asked, "Jack, how are we supposed to get through the Violet Vultures now? We're trapped: they've surrounded us!"

Jack frowned, scratching his head and thinking. "I've no idea, Annie. But we do have the map. Let us see if it can help us now."

He pulled out the map and opened it. They spent a few minutes trying to figure out something from the map, but before their eyes, a few of the mountains on the map started to glow, lighting up with a soft, golden shimmer. Jack asked, confused, "What is happening? Do you have any idea what is going on here?"

Annie stared at the glowing spots and said, "I don't know exactly, but I think it's trying to tell us something important about the Violet Vultures."

Jack's face brightened a little. "Maybe it's like... a sign. A guide to show us the way through this crazy, dangerous place. The Violet Vultures aren't something you cross on your own. We're going to need all the help we can get. Let's take this as our guide!"

With that, the twins knew they had to trust the map, no matter how scary the journey ahead seemed.

Annie, biting her lip, looked at Jack and asked, "But, Jack, what do we do about those violet flowers? They appear to be dangerous as well!"

Jack grinned, taking out a tiny bottle of perfume from his backpack. "Don't worry, look at this! This is the special chocolate cosmos perfume you wanted to bring along. Its smell is strong enough to block out the scent of these flowers. We should be okay if we don't get too close to the flowers. With the help of the map, this perfume, and a little luck, we'll safely make it through the mountains."

Talking less, they both took a deep breath and doused themselves in the unique chocolate cosmos perfume. Glancing at each other, they began their ascent without hesitation.

Amid their courageous climb, a thick mist appeared that defied all attempts to pierce it. Due to the dense atmosphere, they could hardly see their own hands in front of them! They could barely see beyond their arms, their spells futile against the mist's resistance. They couldn't even see the mountains properly!

"How are we going to cross this?" Annie mumbled, her heart pounding like a drum.

Jack squinted through the mist, trying to see the map. "Don't worry, Annie. All we have to do is think smart. We can match what we can see with the map and trust it. Let's give it a try."

So, step by step, the twins made their way through the misty mountains. The mist was thick and creepy, but they didn't give up. Even though they both were nervous, they knew they had to be brave.

Annie's foot slipped, and she almost tumbled off the mountain's edge! She couldn't see anything because of the thick fog. Luckily, their pet frog, Croaky, was hopping along and spotted a knife stuck in the ground! But, being a frog, he couldn't pull it out. So, he transformed back into his human self, using magic to hide himself from Jack and Annie in the fog. He pulled the knife out, enchanted it, and threw it before Jack.

The knife glowed brightly, and the fog magically cleared in a circle. Jack bent down to pick it up, but Annie grabbed his arm.

"Jack, wait!" she warned. "Who knows if this is good or bad? What if you touch it, and it explodes?"

"Annie, I'm going to nudge it with my foot, and we will decide based on the outcome," Jack whispered.

Jack cautiously extended a toe towards the glowing knife and nudged it a few inches forward. The mist instantly vanished from where the knife had cut through it. With a glint of triumph in his eyes, he sliced the fog in front of them like a knife through soft cheese, clearing a path before them.

After a few more knife swipes, they stood at the scariest part of the mountain—The Slide of Death. It was called that because the peak looked like a super sharp wedge and was so steep that one wrong move would send you sliding down straight into a sea of spiky cactuses and jagged rocks. It was crucial to lie on your stomach and crawl along the mountain, or you would slide to your death on cactuses and pointy rocks in an avalanche of violet flowers that would drag along with you yet could not be used as a rope.

The only way to make it across the mountain was by balancing perfectly on the tip of the wedge. Jack and Annie were fortunate when they sliced through the mist and saw the end of the mountain, along with some stone steps leading down. But just as they were about to celebrate, Jack stood up too fast, lost his balance, and slipped off the edge before Annie could even scream!

# 4.
# SWAMP OF THE ANCIENT PREDATOR

Jack vanished down the mountain, but just in time, Annie grabbed his hand before he slipped entirely out of reach. "Hang on, Jack!" she shouted, her heart pounding. Jack clung tightly to the sharp wedge, and Annie, thinking fast, whipped out their rope and made a lasso in seconds. She held onto Jack with one hand and tried to loop the lasso around him, but as she did, she lost her balance! Annie tumbled, but luckily, the lasso caught a sturdy piece of rock just before she fell too far.

Jack grabbed onto the bottom of the lasso while Annie, gritting her teeth, pulled herself back up. Then, with all her strength, she stretched out her hand and yanked Jack onto the wedge again. They scrambled the rest of the way to the end of the mountain range, their hearts racing. They were stunned into silence, frightened out of their wits.

Once they had safely reached the ground, they sat down, still shaking from the terrifying climb. It took them a few minutes to gather their thoughts and understand what had happened.

After they'd rested well and were ready to tackle the next part of their journey, Jack and Annie were about to head out when they spotted a swamp ahead of them. It was gross—a bubbling, smelly mess of squishy mud with stinky, rotten egg fumes rising from it. They stopped in their tracks, trying to figure out how on earth they'd get across this.

Then, out of nowhere, Annie saw something moving in the swamp. "Jack, look!" she whispered, her eyes wide and her face stunned.

"What? There's nothing there," Jack said, squinting at the swamp like he thought Annie was seeing things.

"Never mind," Annie replied, shaking her head. "Let's just focus on this swamp for now."

But a few minutes later, three, maybe four, things started moving in the swamp, sloshing around like shadows under the yucky water. They weren't close together anymore; they were spread out like circling.

Jack's eyes widened, and he yelled, "I saw it too!"

"Do you know what it could be?" Annie whispered, her heart thudding in her chest.

"Do you have any idea what it could be?" Annie asked, still whispering.

Jack frowned. "No, but I have a few guesses, and none are good."

They were so busy talking that they overlooked one of the things getting super close. Then, out of nowhere, they all shot up from the swamp, splashing water everywhere. The creatures finally revealed themselves: crocodiles! Big, mean-looking crocs. The realization hit them both like a thunderbolt, their hearts pounding.

The crocs were closing in, their sharp teeth glinting in the murky water. Annie and Jack knew they couldn't risk waiting without a second thought. They stretched out their fingers, muttered a quick sleeping spell they'd learned, and—poof—the crocodiles slumped into the water, fast asleep.

Phew!

Then, working together, Annie and Jack heaved the crocodiles (they were SO heavy!) and tossed them into the swamp, lining them up like stepping stones. One by one, they jumped from croc to croc, trying not to slip. When they finally reached the other side, they took off running as fast as their legs could carry them, just in case the crocodiles woke up! After what felt like forever, they collapsed many miles away, safely on the ground. They munched on their never-ending bread and water, laughing and catching their breath. Then, at the same time, Annie and Jack yelled, "THAT WAS FUN!"

After munching on their never-ending bread, they checked the map for their next stop. Jack squinted at it and asked, "Annie, where do we go now?"

"According to the map, we need to head north!" she replied, carefully examining the map.

So, they set off on their adventure, trudging another few kilometres north until they finally reached their next stop. They traversed the final stretch of the day, entering a field that, as the map indicated, harboured a concealed trapdoor amidst its grassy expanse. The field looked straight out of a storybook, with grass swaying gently in the breeze and wildflowers dancing everywhere. Jack looked around, scratching his head. "Where could this trapdoor be?" he wondered, scanning the ground for any signs of the hidden door.

"It's hidden, Jack! If we want to find this trapdoor, we've got to start looking!"

With that, they began their search, scouring closely at the ground for any signs of hinges or shiny metal rings. Suddenly, Annie felt her foot get caught on something and stumbled forward. When she looked down, she saw that a metal ring from the trapdoor had caught her foot!

"Jack! Look!" she shouted, her heart racing with excitement and a little bit of fear.

Together, they knelt and started to clear away the grass. Before long, Jack's fingers brushed against something cold and shiny. He hurriedly pushed the grass aside, and there it was—the trapdoor, just waiting to be opened! They leaned in closer, their hearts pounding like drums, sensing that this door was not ordinary.

It was made of shiny metal, and the ring was sparkling gold. There were unicorns all over it, looking magical and beautiful. As soon as they found it, Jack and Annie tried using their magic and the knife they used to slice the mist to pry it open, but nothing worked. They even wished for a crowbar to help, but that just bent and twisted like a pretzel!

Then, Croaky got a clever idea. But he must put Jack and Annie under a sleeping spell to pull it off. So he did!

A few minutes later, Jack and Annie yawned at the same time. Jack rubbed his eyes and said in a voice heavy with sleep, "I suddenly feel super sleepy. It's like something is forcing me to sleep!"

"Me too, Jack! I... barely... barely... bar… zzzzzzzzzzzzzzzzzzzzzzzzz zzzzzz."

Annie couldn't finish her sentence and flopped to the ground, fast asleep. Jack could barely whisper, "Annie, wake up, please. Wake… up… please… please… plzzzzzzzzzzzzzzzzzzzzzzzzzzzzzzz."

Meanwhile, having put them both to sleep, their clever little frog cracked his knuckles and got to work. First, he conjured up a bush to hide behind and transformed into his human form.

Then he tried a prying spell. He waved his hands and shouted the magic words, but it bounced off the trapdoor and landed far back. Undeterred, he tried a lifting spell next, but the trapdoor just gobbled it up like it was a snack!

Finally, he resorted to his last option. His face became a mask of concentration. He raised his hands above the trapdoor and held them there for what felt like forever! After a long time, his determined hard work paid off. With a little bit of magic and determination, he finally opened the trapdoor and even oiled it to make it creak less. It was a tiny victory but a big deal in their grand adventure!

As the sleepy spell lifted, Annie stirred awake, her body feeling achy and weird from the deep slumber. She nudged Jack and blinked a few times. "Hey, do you have any idea how we just dozed off like that?" she asked, her confused voice. "It wasn't like our usual sleep!" She looked around, remembering what had happened before they nodded off. What was going on?

Jack, still feeling sleepy and fuzzy, shook his head in response. Annie, curious and excited, decided to try the trapdoor again. To her astonishment, it swung open super easily, devoid of the usual resistance.

Jack rubbed his eyes and blinked in disbelief. "What in the world...? Just a second ago, it was rusty and wouldn't budge! Now it's as smooth as butter! Something's amiss here."

Annie thought for a moment, her eyes shining. "Maybe it's because I made a wish in my dream that the trapdoor would open! Do you think my wish came true?"

It was super quiet when they opened the trapdoor, like a secret hideout. Inside, it was pitch dark, and they could see some steps made of squishy soil leading down into the shadows. Annie and Jack quickly grabbed their torches and turned them on, lighting up the way ahead.

As they carefully descended the stairs, they spotted squirmy worms wiggling around in the dirt. "Ew!" Annie giggled, trying to avoid stepping on any of them.

But then, at the end of the stairs, they slipped right into a muddy puddle! SPLAT! Suddenly, Annie's arms got all tangled around Jack's legs, and one of Jack's arms ended up wrapped around Annie's neck like a goofy hug.

"Whoa! This is not how I imagined our adventure would go!" Jack laughed, trying to untangle himself.

When they finally reached some flat ground, Annie and Jack heard spooky growls and strange scrapes echoing around them, but when they looked around, nothing was there. It was just their imaginations playing tricks! Or was it?

As they kept walking, they found themselves in an endless tunnel. It was dark and creepy, and after what seemed like ages, Jack's tired voice broke the silence. “Annie, this tunnel is like a never-ending piece of string. I’m so tired. Can we please take a break for the night?”

“Yeah, Jack,” Annie agreed, yawning. “Let’s call it a day and set up camp here!”

They quickly got to work, pulling out their sleeping bags and a tent, ready to rest.

After a long, hectic day, they were finally relieved to sleep in their tent. Nothing scary or weird happened, or at least that’s what it seemed like. Just as they had fallen asleep, a creepy monster—like something from your worst nightmares—crept out of its dark lair. And the beast sniffed them out. Its presence gave them goosebumps, even though they were still asleep. Something felt off, and it sent cold shivers down their spines.

But luckily, they woke up just in time! The monster’s loud growls woke them up. Without wasting a second, they took off running as fast as their legs could carry them. As they dashed through the dark, twisty tunnel, Annie panted, “Jack... do you think... this is the... right way?”

Just as out of breath, Jack replied, “I... don’t know... Annie... but we... have to... get away from... whatever’s... chasing us!”

They kept running, unsure if they were heading the right way, but feeling they were. The tunnel was so dark that they could barely see anything, and their hearts were pounding in their chests. Just when they thought they might escape, they stumbled upon the monster, its massive form filling their vision.

Its giant body filled the entire tunnel, and slowly, it turned its colossal head toward them. The deep, low growl from its throat was so terrifying that it made their bodies shake with fear.

# 5.
# UNSHACKLED WINGS

Jack and Annie found themselves rooted to the spot, their hearts pounding in their chests as they laid eyes on the creature. It was no ordinary monster but a colossal dragon, its body ablaze with a fiery yellow-orange hue. Its back was a menacing sight, adorned with spikes in shades of green and blue. Like a warning flag, a red frill fluttered behind its foxlike ears. When it opened its maw, a torrent of orange flames burst forth, revealing teeth as sharp as the stalactites and stalagmites of a cave. It moved with an eerily human-like gait, its claws gleaming like swords, ready to strike.

The dragon's fiery gaze locked onto Jack and Annie, and terror washed over them. Jack, who had delved into ancient legends, felt a shiver of recognition. He leaned over to Annie and whispered, his voice shaking, "Annie, do you think this could be the dragon from that old legend? The one that, if you say its name five times, it comes with you? I've never read what it looks like, but I know it's super powerful and unpredictable."

"It might be, Jack. But if it's not the dragon from the legend, we'll need something to fight our way past it," Annie said, biting her lip.

Jack nodded nervously. "Annie, if we're not sure, maybe we should try it."

"You're right, Jack. Fingers crossed this works."

Together, they took a deep breath and shouted at the same time, "Flame, Flame, Flame, Flame, Flame!"

But oh no! They got the name wrong! The dragon let out a deafening roar and shot a searing blast of flames towards them. The fire hit the rock they were hiding behind, sending thick smoke everywhere. Jack and Annie, their hearts racing, scrambled towards the nearest boulder, their fear palpable.

Panicked, they quickly picked a new name and yelled as loud as they could, "Poof, Poof, Poof, Poof, Poof!"

But guess what? That name was wrong, too! Looking super annoyed now, the dragon blasted more flames at the rock, covering everything in thick smoke again. The dragon, seemingly exasperated, let out a huff of smoke as if to say, 'Really? Another wrong guess?' Jack and Annie could almost feel the dragon rolling its eyes at them!

"Wait, Jack! Look at all that smoke coming out of its nostrils," Annie whispered, eyes wide. "What if its name is Smoky? We should try it! As per the legend, if you guess a dragon's real name, you have power over it. If we can guess its name, we might control it... and escape from here!" Annie's voice shook, a mix of fear and hope that they could pull it off.

"Annie, we can't wait any longer! The dragon is growing more enraged by the second!" Jack said, his voice is serious and determined. "We need to try saying 'Smoky' to it and do it now!"

He pointed at the dragon, which was stomping and breathing fire everywhere. Annie nodded quickly, her heart racing. "You know what? 'Smoky' really suits him! With all that smoke coming from his nose, his name has to be something like Smoky... or maybe it is Smoky!"

Stomp! Stomp! Stomp! The dragon thundered down the tunnel, shaking the ground like an earthquake. Its fiery eyes blazed with anger as it turned to face them, getting closer and closer. Jack and Annie held their breath, thinking they were about to be roasted like marshmallows over a campfire.

But then, to their surprise, the dragon's fierce face broke into a big, toothy smile! "How in the world did you know my name?" it boomed, a mix of surprise and amusement.

Jack and Annie exchanged wide-eyed glances, a wave of relief washing over them like a warm blanket. They couldn't believe it! "Wait a minute... You're Smoky? Thank goodness! Now we can say that some legends are true!" Annie squealed, bouncing on her toes.

With a sense of accomplishment, Jack said, "Well, now that Smoky's our friend, maybe we can ask him to help us get out of this tunnel!" He turned to Smoky with a mischievous glint in his eyes, like he was always up to something fun.

Smoky nodded with a smirk and said, "Follow me," in a playful voice, like he had a secret they didn't know yet. He stood up, his big dragon feet thudding softly on the ground, and started walking ahead.

Jack and Annie exchanged excited glances. The plan was simple now—follow Smoky, the dragon who knew every twist and turn of this dark tunnel. Maybe they'd find their way out with some dragon help!

So, they started walking towards the exit, excited because they could see the grassy plain on the other side. It was full of wildflowers, with sunshine pouring down and a nice breeze blowing—it looked perfect, like a dream! But just when Jack and Annie were about to step through, the exit pushed them backwards like they hit an invisible wall!

They tried everything. They fired different spells at the exit—zap, zap, zap! But nope, the exit just bounced them right back! Smoky tried shooting fire at the exit, but it didn't work either. It was like the exit was laughing at them or something. With a thoughtful look on his dragon face, Smoky said, "Hmm... how about I shoot my fire, and you two shoot your spells simultaneously? Maybe if we all attack together, we can beat it!"

"Well, I suppose we could try it," Jack said, scratching his head. "But if it doesn't work, we need a Plan B. What do you say, Annie?"

Annie thought for a while; then her eyes lit up. "I know! We can use the wish soil for Plan B to wish the enchantment away. But let's try Smoky's idea first, of course!"

"All right, that seems like a plan!" Jack grinned.

Smoky stomped his foot, ready for action. "Okay, you two have decided. On the count of three, I'll blast my fire, and you both use your spells. Ready? One... two... three!"

Simultaneously, Smoky let forth a fiery blast while Jack and Annie fired their spells, hoping it would finally break the implacable exit!

Smoky blasted fire from his mouth, and Annie and Jack shot their spells as hard as possible. The enchantment finally cracked after what felt like forever—roaring flames and bright flashes everywhere! It shattered like a broken mirror, and the exit was clear.

At that exact moment, far away, a wicked witch felt a strange buzz run through her body. She froze mid-step, her eyes narrowing as she paced up and down her lair. But now, she realized something was off. "Someone has freed Smoky," she muttered with a growl.

Smoky stretched his enormous wings and yawned as soon as they walked into the sunlight. "Is there any food around? I am starving!" he grumbled, his stomach rumbling like thunder.

Jack and Annie looked at each other, surprised and worried. "Uh, of course, Smoky! We'll give you something to eat!" they said together quickly.

It was funny—who would've thought a giant, fire-breathing dragon would say something like this? But they knew one thing for sure: they definitely couldn't refuse!

As Jack and Annie rummaged through their bag for food for Smoky, a scroll tumbled out, along with some bacon and eggs. After taking a whiff of the food, Smoky devoured it all in one sitting. "Mmm, delicious! But what's that thing?" he inquired, gesturing with his paw to the paper.

Jack looked at the scroll and said, "Oh, this? It's a scroll about a fairy tale. You read it to learn stuff and for entertainment, Smoky."

Annie pleaded, her voice tinged with exhaustion and anxiety, "We're so tired and cranky right now. Could you kindly watch over us while we sleep? Just in case something creepy shows up?"

Smoky smiled, "Obviously! You rest. I'll watch out that nothing ambushes us. However, guarding can get extremely boring, especially when there's no action. Can I read that scroll while you two snooze? It'll help me stay awake!"

Rubbing his eyes, Jack said, "Yeah, Smoky, go ahead, but be super careful, okay? Don't, like, accidentally tear it with your claws. This scroll is precious!"

With a warm smile on his face, Smoky flashed his pointed teeth. "Don't worry, Jack. I'll be as amiable as a kitten," he promised, picking up the scroll with the tip of his claws like it was the most delicate thing ever.

Jack and Annie set up camp, their bodies weary from the day's journey, but their hearts brimming with excitement and trepidation. Smoky, deliberate and cautious, unfurled the scroll and began to read. Their fatigue faded as the two kids rested, giving way to a buzzing sense of adventure. With curiosity and caution, Annie looked up at Smoky and asked, "Where did you come from?"

Smoky paused, looking thoughtful, and then, with a melancholy smile, said, "That, my little friends, is quite the story..."

Smoky cleared his throat and began to speak, "I used to live inside a river once. One day, I was just a little dragon kid, snoozing, when I was startled awake by something strange. I swam to the river's surface, and suddenly, there was a flash of bright light, and my eyes shut. When I opened them... whoosh! I was inside that trapdoor tunnel!

"The worst part? I wanted to call for help, but I couldn't even talk. My voice was gone until someone finally set me free. And no matter how many times and how hard I try to get out of that tunnel, it would just push me back like, 'Nope, you're staying here.' So, I was stuck there for... well, I don't know how long. That's all I can remember." Jack and Annie were listening intently as he sighed and seemed thoughtful.

Smoky's mysterious past piqued their curiosity, leaving them eager to uncover more. It was like a treasure map; they were ready to explore every clue! All of a sudden, Smoky's eyes lit up like fireworks.

"Wait a minute... what?! I had parents?" he exclaimed, looking shocked. "This isn't my home? Whoa, that's a new thing!"

You might be wondering why the witch took away Smoky's speaking ability. If she hadn't, he would've been shouting for help so loud that the whole world would have heard him! Dragons have voices like thunder.

# 6.
# THE LAND OF SLEEPINESS

After discussing Smoky's past, they ascended a hill, their footsteps resonating in the stillness. When they finally reached the top, they gasped in stupefaction! It was like stepping into an incredible work of art!

A vast expanse of flowers, a vibrant tapestry of colours, extended as far as the eye could see.

Below them spread a gigantic sea of flowers, splashing colours everywhere—reds, yellows, purples, and blues danced together in the sunshine. Jack's eyes widened in awe. He turned to Annie, practically bouncing on his toes. "Annie, what in the world is that?!" he shouted. "I've never seen such a kaleidoscope of nature! It looks like a rainbow threw up everywhere!"

"Neither have I, Jack," she murmured, her tone a mixture of wonder and concern. "Maybe we should check the map to see if this is our next challenge."

They pulled out the map, and right there, a red upside-down teardrop popped up over a big patch of super bright orange flowers. The words "The Land of Sleepiness" danced around it. The flowers looked beautiful and inviting, almost like they whispered, "Come play with us!"

Jack's voice bubbled with a mix of excitement and caution. "Annie, this must be our next stop! The Land of Sleepiness! I can't help but imagine the adventures and dangers that await us there. What do you think we'll have to encounter here?" He grinned, his imagination running wild as they stared at the map.

Annie nodded, feeling a tingle of adventure in her tummy. "Yeah, let's do it! But we need to be careful."

So, with Smoky trailing behind them and chatting away with the inquisitive little frog, they carefully descended the hill. The flowers wobbled gently in the breeze, as if waving hello. As they entered The Land of Sleepiness, Jack felt a thrill rush through him.

As they stepped closer, the flowers looked even more magical. Their bright orange petals were shaped like tiny cups, each holding a sprinkle of red pollen. The pollen danced in the breeze, swirling around like little fairy dust, making Jack, Annie, and Smoky feel a tickle in their noses. "Achoo!" went Jack, followed by Annie and Smoky, all sneezing in a chorus.

"Wow, these flowers are gorgeous! But do you think The Land of Sleepiness is sleepy?" Jack asked, his eyes sparkling with curiosity.

Annie frowned a bit, her voice sounding a little worried. "I do wonder, Jack, but I am afraid we don't have time to find out. The sun is starting to set, and the predators may come out with it! We must haste to avoid being trapped in The Land of Sleepiness."

With a determined nod, they quickened their pace, ready to face whatever lay ahead in The Land of Sleepiness.

"The flowers in this land are not just beautiful," Smoky said, his eyes wide and earnest. "They're lethal! Their fragrance can lull you into a slumber you may never awaken from. It's a risk we can't afford to take."

Jack and Annie exchanged glances, their mouths wide open in surprise. "Whoa! How do you know all this, Smoky?" they enquired simultaneously, their voices filled with marvel.

Smoky puffed out his chest a little, looking proud. "Well, I've been around for a long time and know a lot about magical plants. And some legends say that if you breathe in too much of this scent, you could end up in a dreamy land for eternity! So we have to be very careful! Now, do you want to see it for yourself?"

"Yeah, Smoky, let's try-even Jack!" Annie chimed in, her eyes darting around, feeling the sleepy vibes of the flowers around her.

"Then let's try it!" stated Smoky. But as soon as they set foot into The Land of Sleepiness, a wave of wearyness washed over them like a fluffy cloud. Jack and Annie stepped back just in time.

"Smoky, maybe you can fly us over these sleepy flowers!" Jack suggested his heart was racing.

"Hmm, maybe. But I'm loving my freedom right now," Smoky said, looking around with a big smile.

Jack scratched his head, curious. "How did you not go completely insane being stuck there for God know how many years?"

Smoky chuckled. "I had my ways! I drew all sorts of things in the dirt, made little balls out of the soil, and spent my days dreaming about when I would be free. I knew it would happen one day!" His eyes glistened with memories of those long, tranquil days.

They were so engrossed in their chat that they didn't see Annie edging nearer to one of the flowers. Suddenly, the flower spun, creating a whirling pattern resembling a magnificent rainbow. It felt like the flower was singing a lullaby specifically for her! Annie leaned in, fascinated, when she took a deep breath, and all the pollen vanished up her nose!

She was immediately jerked out of her trance-like state. Her head spun like a merry-go-round, and colourful sparkles danced before her eyes. Her knees felt like jelly, and she began to sway like a tree in a storm.

Jack gave her a wide-eyed stare. "What's wrong, Annie?" he asked worriedly.

Jack didn't get an answer and instead heard a loud THUD! He saw that Annie had given up on trying to stand and plopped down on the ground, falling next to a sleepy frog.

"Annie!" Jack yelled and rushed over. He bent down to lift her, but she felt as heavy as a big rock! Jack's heart pounded as he realized he had no choice but to wait for Smoky.

"Smoky! Help!" he loudly cried, his voice booming through the air.

Smoky heard him and lunged in. His eyes grew wide when he realized what had happened. He slung Annie and the frog over his shoulders without thinking much and made Jack sit on his back. "Hold on tight!" he said, flying over the Land of Sleepiness.

With a mighty flap of his wings, Smoky took off into the sky, far above The Land of Sleepiness. The warm breeze rushed past them, and Jack felt great ease. They had escaped the grips of the creepy, sleepy flowers, and it felt like a big win!

After flying for a long time, they dashed out of The Land of Sleepiness. They landed by a shimmering river where Smoky used to live before that annoying witch had snatched him away to guard her trapdoor. The water glimmered in the sunlight, and Smoky gently put Jack and Annie down on a cosy bed of rushes he had made just for them.

"All right, time for a little adventure!" Smoky said as Jack climbed back onto his back. Smoky took off with a powerful flutter of his mighty wings, soaring high above the river to see if they could fly across. However, as they reached the middle, something peculiar happened. It felt like they had hit an invisible barrier!

"Uh-oh," Jack said, feeling a bit nervous. "What's going on?"

"I can't fly any further! It's like there's some barrier!" Smoky replied, flapping his wings in frustration.

With no choice, they returned to the riverbank where they had left Annie and the frog. Once they touched down, Smoky took out the toolbox. "Let's see if we can make a boat!" he said enthusiastically.

Jack nodded, remembering how they had taught Smoky to make things. Together, they wished for some sturdy wood planks. As the planks magically appeared, they got to work, hammering and tying things together. With some teamwork, they were ready to create their own boat to sail across the river!

Meanwhile, Jack and Smoky were busy working on the boat while Annie snoozed away peacefully. Smoky knew the flowers would keep her sleepy for a while, so he took the chance to get things ready for their next obstacle. It's always best to be prepared for whatever tricky stuff might come their way—especially with Jack, the strategy master!

After about an hour, Annie finally stirred. She rubbed her eyes and yawned so loudly that it sounded like a bear emerging from hibernation! Jack and Smoky both turned to stare at her, forgetting what they were doing.

"Where am I? What is this place? How did I come here, Smoky?" Annie asked, still dazed as she looked at the gorgeous landscape around her.

"You're back beside the river, outside the border of The Land of Sleepiness, Annie! We're making a boat to cross it," Jack replied, trying to squelch a giggle at how comical she looked, all weary and perplexed.

Smoky looked at Annie seriously, saying, "I picked you up and carried you on my shoulder, along with Jack and Croaky, to get you all out of there safely. You see, dragons are unaffected by such dangerous flowery smells. They're super cunning!"

He paused momentarily, then continued, "You should lie back and rest while Jack and I finish making this boat. That scent can make anyone sick, and we want you to be fantastic for the next leg of our adventure!"

Annie nodded, acknowledging how exhausted she still felt. "Okay, Smoky," she said, lying back on the soft rushes. "You guys conclude the boat. I'll be all set to join you in no time!"

She closed her eyes, listening to the sounds of the river and her friends working hard nearby, feeling secure and excited about the adventures still ahead.

Annie, still a little sleepy but curious, questioned, "Wait, Smoky, why do we need a boat? Can't you fly us over the river?"

Smoky gasped and shook his head. "I wish it were that simple, Annie. But the witch has put up strong magic wards around the river. They're imperceptible barriers which can't be flown over. We can cross the river the old-fashioned way—with a boat!"

Annie frowned, "Wow, that witch is clever, huh?"

Smoky chuckled, "Yes! But we'll outwit her, don't worry. This boat will get us across, and we'll keep moving forward!"

Now, you're probably thinking, Why did the frog fall asleep, too, right? Well, here's the deal. See, this wasn't just an ordinary frog. Nope! He was a wizard hiding in the form of a frog. And for that reason, he had to behave like a frog, or else he'd revert to his original self. The truth is, the flowers didn't trouble him. He was an experienced wizard and could handle magic like that. The real reason he fell asleep? His magic energy was depleted, and he needed a nap to recharge.

Anyway, where had I been? Oh yeah! After a little while, the frog began to stir and started ribbiting. Annie saw him, smiled, and took him gently in her hands.

Annie and Jack didn't know much about the frog, but one thing was sure: he was the smartest frog they had ever seen! He could read, understand what they were saying, and even gave little signals to show how he felt. Sometimes, he'd shake his head yes or no, just like a person! Jack smiled and said, "Once Smoky and I finish this boat, we'll all have supper together."

So, after a long, tiring day, they all had their supper outside under the sky, and when the sun finally set, and the boat was complete, they decided to take turns, just in case any dreadful dangers crept out from The Land of Sleepiness. Smoky took the first shift, standing guard outside the little tent they had constructed. It wasn't a fancy tent or anything – just a blanket draped over some sticks – but it was hot inside.

They were so occupied with all the hustling and bustling that they didn't notice how fast time passed. The sun had already begun to rise over the horizon by the time they finally managed to get a decent night's sleep. But it didn't last long—Jack woke them up after only a few hours. Everyone groaned a bit, but they knew they had to keep going. After breakfast, they sat in their boat and began to cross the river.

Everything seemed fine at first, but just as they reached the middle of the river—SPLASH! A massive wave came out of nowhere and soaked them all from head to toe! Their clothes were dripping, and they shivered like wet puppies.

# 7.
# BLAZE OF REUNION

Right after the wave soaked them, a vast roar shook the air. It was so loud that it even reverberated to the witch's castle. The witch sneered to herself, thinking, Good. Smoky's family must be dealing with any bothersome strangers who dared to cross the river.

Jack and Annie rubbed the water from their eyes, and when they finally looked up, their jaws dropped. Right in front of them stood a whole dragon family! They looked just like Smoky but more significant—a lot bigger. There were two giant dragons, a mama and papa, and beside them, two little dragons that looked like mini versions of Smoky.

The papa dragon glared down at them, his voice roaring, "This is our river! Get out now, or we'll eat you up, and no one will ever know you were here!"

Jack and Annie froze. What could they possibly do now?

Smoky suddenly jumped before Jack and Annie, standing tall and brave. He snarled at the big dragons, "You won't touch them! If you do, I'll turn you all into ashes!"

The papa dragon squinted at Smoky, tilting his big dragon head. "You look and sound like us, and you've got our courage. Before we roast you, please tell us who and where you're from. We're curious to know."

Without missing a beat, Smoky shot back, "I'm a water-dragon. I was taken away from my parents, and I haven't seen them since. Are you satisfied now? If so, will you let us cross the river?"

The air was so tense that you could practically hear their hearts thumping.

Suddenly, all four dragons gasped—like a HUGE gasp! The papa dragon's voice started to shake. "S-Smoky? Is it you? Have you finally come back to us, to your family?"

Smoky's eyes got wide, and his voice trembled as he spoke. "M-Mom? Dad? Is it you?"

"Of course, it's us, our dear Smoky!" his mom said, her voice soft but excited. "We thought we'd lost you forever! Come on now, won't you give your parents a big bear hug?"

Smoky's heart was racing. Could this be happening? His family... right here?

Before they even finished speaking, Smoky flew right into their arms, hugging them so tight that it wrinkled their scaly skin. He was so happy, he didn't want to let go. After a moment, Smoky looked at the two smaller dragons standing beside his parents and asked, "And who are you two?"

The little girl dragon spoke up first, "I'm your younger sister, Saffire!" she said, puffing her chest out proudly. Then the little boy dragon added, "And I'm your brother, Sefyr!"

Smoky smiled and explained everything to his family—the kidnapping incident, how he got stuck guarding the trapdoor for the witch, and all about Jack and Annie's adventure. He told them where they were headed and how he was helping them.

After talking for what felt like forever, Smoky finally asked, "Mom, Dad, what's the best way to get to the witch's castle?"

Papa Dragon growled, "We're coming with you. That witch took you from us, and we've been waiting for the day we could take our revenge!"

The whole dragon family joined the crew as they crossed the river. When they reached the middle, something caught Jack's eye. There, on a tiny island, were a bunch of caves huddled together like little stone houses. Right in the middle of the island was an old well with a roof, but it was shaped like a funnel, and its hole was minuscule, so only rainwater could fall into it.

Jack pointed excitedly and said, "Look over there! An island! Maybe we'll find something useful there!"

While swimming next to the boat, Smoky and his family helped guide it towards the island. Jack kept insisting they stop there, so they finally did. The island was small but super cool. All sorts of plants were growing everywhere, and the sun was shining so hot that you almost wanted to just lie under a tree and take a nap. But no, there was exploring to do!

The trees were mainly palm trees, and the lake sparkled with numerous small creatures swimming around, including a flock of aquatic creatures called flippernapplekers. They had scrummylicious jelly inside their bones, and you had to roast them on a spit to get the jelly out of them. Flippernappleker-jelly was a very popular dessert in Sleepyfield. Jack, Annie, Smoky, and the dragons wandered around until they peeked into one of the caves.

Suddenly, before they even had time to blink, they were surrounded! Men, women, and even kids popped out of nowhere, all pointing sharp arrows at their necks!

# 8.
# UNITED BY WRATH

The tribals looked wild! They wore animal skins and leaves, with the men sporting headgear made from plants. The women wore necklaces made of bones and teeth, which looked super spooky, and even the kids had miniature bows and arrows aimed right at them.

Jack and Annie felt anxious as the tribals waggled their hands and stepped closer. They both turned to Smoky and whispered, "Do you know who these tribals are?"

Smoky shook his head and muttered, "I don't know anyone here."

Jack and Annie glanced at each other, thinking the same thing at the same time: "Oh no! We are in a pickle now!"

Suddenly, this massive, bulky man burst out of the crowd. He was the chief because he had this enormous crown of leaves and grass that looked too big for his head. He boomed, "What in the world is going on here? I told you all to get ready! It's almost hunting time, and you are not honing the tools!"

But before he even saw Smoky, Smoky's eyes fell on him. Smoky called out, "Wiseman? Is that you? I thought you left on a journey a long time ago!"

To everyone's surprise, Wiseman blinked and said, "Smoky? After all these years?"

Everyone was stunned when Wiseman and Smoky unexpectedly embraced like long-lost friends. Wiseman quickly turned to the tribals and said, "Release them! It's Q-time, and I'm starting it right now!"

(By the way, Q-time means Question Time— I just thought you should know!)

The tribals guided Jack, Annie, and Smoky to this small, squishy clay and mud hut. The sign on the front said: THE Q-TIME HUT. It was so tiny that Smoky had to cram in, and even then, his wings got stuck in the door!

Wiseman waved them to some floor mats while the tribals stayed outside, trying to listen through the walls. Jack and Annie sat down, and Smoky curled up as much as he could.

Wiseman crossed his arms and said, "All right, spill it. What brings you here? Why do you have dragons with you? Are they the servants of the witch? And did she send you to cause more trouble for us?"

Jack, Annie, and Smoky glanced at each other, knowing they had much to explain!

Annie whispered to Jack as she came close, "Do you think we should tell them? They do not look like they are on the witch's side."

Jack nodded slightly, whispering back, "Maybe we should, Annie. It seems like the witch has been bothering them, too."

Annie took a deep breath and started to explain everything. "Okay, here's what happened. A powerful storm came and washed away all the money in our village. We lost everything! We assumed that we would come here to locate the treasure rumoured to be hidden in the witch's castle. The storm took our money; we hope the treasure can help us regain it. But to get here, we've had to travel the world's most treacherous mountain range, go through a crocodile-infested swamp, and even escape The Land of Sleepiness! It's been a wild adventure so far!"

Jack and Annie looked at Wiseman, waiting to see if he'd believe their story.

After Annie finished explaining, Wiseman's countenance grew serious. "All these years," he said, his voice grave, "the witch has been robbing our food. To take what little we have, she sends her storms and hordes. Things are so bad that we barely have enough to survive, and our tribe is shrinking! We will join you on your quest. We need retribution, and we'll get it by using our arrows to end her once and for all."

Annie frowned and said, "But why are you so desperate for vengeance? I don't mean to offend, but what has she done to you that makes you want to...you know...destroy her? Even that is something neither Jack nor I wish to accomplish, and her storm took everything from our village!"

Wiseman sighed profoundly and glanced at his people. "It's a long and unfortunate story. My fellow tribespeople, do you want me to tell these strangers the story of our decline? So they understand why we have to put an end to her?"

Murmurs of "Yes" trickled through the crowd like the wind through leaves. It seemed that this was a heavy burden the tribespeople had to unload to continue, as they had been carrying it for too long.

Wiseman moaned and said, "Well then, get ready for a true emotional rollercoaster. After I tell you about our miserable downfall, you must explain your plans for the witch's castle."

He took a deep breath and started, "Not too long ago, we lived in a village called Eternal Haven. It was exquisite. Our homes were sturdy, there were trees everywhere, schools for the children, and even our police force. Everything you could think of to make life ideal. We had plenty of food and fresh water, and everyone had a place to stay. The whole village gleamed with cleanliness."

Wiseman paused momentarily, his eyes distant as if remembering the village that once stood proud.

"We were living happily in Eternal Haven when one day, out of nowhere, black paper bits started falling from the sky," Wiseman continued, his voice growing more intense. "At first, we were not sure what was happening, but they didn't fall for long. Then, BOOM! A tremendous storm hit, more powerful than anything we'd ever seen. Our homes were shattered, and even our carts got flushed into the river."

Jack and Annie leaned in, eyes wide, as Wiseman went on. "And that's not all. The witch—her sorcery contaminated our river. The only clean water left was in our special well, the Everwell. So, in the middle of the storm, we grabbed whatever scrap metal we could find to build a barrier around it. Yet that wasn't a formidable barrier. Thank goodness the storm didn't touch our Everwell, or we would have lost everything."

He sighed, his voice quivering a bit. "After the storm ceased, all you could see was a mess of straw, clay, and mud. Then something weird happened. As black as the midnight sky, a midnight swan descended from above. It landed right in front of us, and an old lady got off its back. It was her. The witch."

Jack shuddered, and Annie clutched her hands together, listening intently.

"The witch just looked at us, all shocked and scared, and she laughed," Wiseman remarked, shaking his head. "'Look at you idiots, grovelling at my feet,' she exclaimed. Then, she presented us with two unappealing choices. She threatened to take all of our food or all of our children to serve as her slaves. If we refused both, she'd feed us all to her chupacabra and blood demon."

Everyone fell silent, the weight of the witch's viciousness sinking in.

Wiseman's voice grew stern as he continued, "I couldn't just stand there and let her take our kids! So, I marched straight up to her and exclaimed, 'No way, witch! Are our kids becoming your slaves? You already destroyed our village and took away everything we had, and now you believe we'll do what you say? N-O spells no!'"

Annie gasped, her eyes wide with admiration for Wiseman's courage.

"But," Wiseman continued, his voice trailing, "the witch didn't flinch. She lifted her hands, and instantly, all of our food—every single piece—started flying out from what was left of our houses. It all zoomed through the air, swirling around her in a giant heap."

Jack's jaw dropped. "What happened next?" he asked, hardly able to control himself.

"With a snap of her fingers," Wiseman said, "the whole heap of food vanished, just like that. Gone. Then she climbed back onto that eerie midnight swan, and before we knew it, she was gone with a piercing screech from the swan and that ghastly cackling laugh from the witch. Just like that."

Everyone sat in silence, stunned by the story.

Wiseman let out a long sigh, his shoulders slumping as he spoke. "After the witch left, we had no choice but to fix what was left of our village. It took days. We used the rubble to build caves and huts—anything we could. Once everything was sort of back to normal, I knew we couldn't wait for the witch to return with those horrible creatures she threatened us with. So, I dug out my old scroll about beasts, and there they were: the chupacabra and the blood demon, nasty creatures. I read everything about defeating them, and then I started training our best fighters, just in case. The witch has kept us scared and weak, taking our food and ensuring we could never rise against her. That's why we've been stuck like this for so long."

Jack's face lit up with determination as he jumped in. "Witch's castle has a treasure, and we aim for it! She sent a storm that took away all our money, and if we obtain that treasure, we can retrieve it. Everything will return to normal again!"

The Wiseman nodded, listening carefully to what Jack said. "We both want revenge on the witch," he addressed everyone. "We ought to cooperate. But we'll need a bigger boat—or even better, a ship—to carry all of us. My men will construct it, and in the meantime, you can all relax and get prepared for the journey ahead."

Then, he turned to the tribals, crossed his eyes several times (which looked pretty funny), and a few of them flared their noses back at him like it was some secret signal! After some time, everyone worked together, and Jack, Annie, Smoky, and his family watched in awe as the tribals used magic to enhance their little boat. Gradually but surely, it was turning into a real ship!

Wiseman turned back to them and grinned, "Each person here possesses a unique power. Mine? I can communicate with all living things, whether it's a human, animal, or even a tree."

Then, the Wiseman led them to a comfortable little hut made just for guests. It was the perfect place to take a snooze! Jack and Annie were so tired that they flopped onto the cots, and before they knew it, they were out like lights.

The next morning, a little boy with big, curious eyes woke them up. It was still dark outside, and he was twitching on his toes. Jack questioned, rubbing his eyes, "Is the ship ready?"

The boy nodded excitedly. Then he added, "You're going to help us defeat the witch, right? Her storm washed away all my family into the river. You won't just leave us alone, will you?"

Annie sat up, looking serious. "Of course, we won't leave you!" she promised. "We're in this together. We'll make sure the witch pays for what she did!"

Jack and Annie were excited to see a large group of tribal people waiting for them when they stepped outside. "Are you ready?" Wiseman asked as he approached.

They all nodded in response. "Well, then, it's now time to board the ship! Our mission awaits us!" Wiseman announced.

As the sun peeked over the horizon, everyone hopped onto the ship. Jack took charge of the tiller, steering the boat with a big grin. Annie beat a steady rhythm on the drum, ensuring the rowers maintained the right pace. Smoky was perched high up in the crow's nest, watching for any trouble, while his family swam alongside the ship.

Together, they crossed the river, hearts racing with excitement for the journey ahead!

# 9.
# COLOURS OF CHALLENGES

After crossing the river and a brief respite, Jack, Annie, Smoky, and the others spotted an incredibly dense jungle of flowers blocking their way. Right in the middle of it was a path. Wiseman scratched his head and said, "Maybe we can just go through and skip any trouble, right?"

So, they all bravely stepped into the flower jungle. But just then, the flowers suddenly grew TEETH! Yes, actual teeth! And they began snapping at them like little monsters. They all bolted out before the flowers could chomp them to pieces.

Out of breath and freaked out, they realized they couldn't just walk through the flowerbed. They had to deal with it somehow. Each flower had seven petals, and every petal had its own stem. All the stems were woven together, and every petal was a colour from the rainbow—red, orange, yellow, green, blue, indigo, and violet. It was like a rainbow-coloured wall of peril, totally covering the path!

With his heart racing, Jack reached out to touch the red petal. His hand shook as he felt it. The second his fingers brushed the petal, it plucked right off by itself!

A message appeared on the red petal. Jack squinted at the writing and read it out loud: "PHYSICAL: FIGHT A MONSTER." And just like that, a vast, horned demon instantly came charging straight at them! Its red eyes were glowing, and it was super fast!

Before anyone could even blink, Annie pointed her hand at it and whispered some magic words, and a spear spell flew through the air and hit the demon right in the head. The demon let out a roar and collapsed to the ground. A weird buzzing sound surrounded it as it fell, like a swarm of angry bees.

Annie almost missed it, but then, one of the demon's horns popped off and landed right on her foot. She jumped up and yelped in surprise, but suddenly, all the red petals on the flowers disappeared!

Annie was quick to run to the next flower. She grabbed its orange petal and tried to pull it off, but... it wouldn't budge! Jack, Wiseman, and even the frog wanted to help her yank it, but no matter how hard they pulled, the orange petal was stuck!

Smoky and his family rushed over to help, tugging on the orange petal with all their might. They pulled and pulled until even the frog's hands started catching fire! The moment the frog's hands lit up, the petal finally popped free, and everyone tumbled backwards into a big pile on the ground—Annie held the orange petal triumphantly.

The frog, whose hands were still on fire, quickly rubbed them on the grass, and the flames went out. Annie looked at the petal and read aloud: "SOCIAL: AN ACTIVITY THAT REQUIRES MORE THAN ONE PERSON."

Just then, a giant image appeared in the air. It was like watching a movie screen! The picture showed a woman with snow-white hair wearing a sparkly crown. She looked like a princess from a fairytale, with this super mysterious smile. In the background, it looked like some famous kingdom full of tourists wandering around.

Underneath the picture were big glowing letters: "UNJUMBLE THE NAME," and below that were four letters: S-A-L-E.

Annie scratched her head. "Sale? That's weird. But we need to figure it out!"

Annie and Jack thought hard, wrinkling their brows and pacing back and forth. Then, all of a sudden, Annie's face brightened like she'd just cracked the biggest mystery ever.

"I got it!" she exclaimed, her voice filled with excitement. "I think I know this princess! I've heard about her before... her name is Elsa! Look at the letters—'Sale' is just an anagram of 'Elsa'! It fits perfectly!"

As soon as she said it, like magic, all the orange petals vanished from the flowers. No longer nervous, Jack grinned and reached for the yellow petal. He quickly tugged it and plucked it off like he'd been doing it his whole life.

Suddenly, they weren't in front of the flowers anymore. A vast, sparkling forest appeared before their eyes, and right in the middle of it stood a shimmering, majestic unicorn, its mane glowing like the stars.

Jack's hands trembled slightly as he read aloud, "MYTHICAL: PLUCK THE UNICORN'S TAIL WITHOUT DYING, AND IT GORGING YOU THROUGH THE HEART WITH ITS HORN." He stared at the petal.

Both Jack and Annie's eyes widened with fear. The thought of getting stabbed by a unicorn's horn made their legs feel shaky. But they took a deep breath, trying to soothe their racing hearts as they started to step forward.

Then, Wiseman gently grasped their shoulders and pulled them back a little. Leaning in close, he whispered, "Unicorns are scared of humans. If more than one of you approaches, it'll think you're a menace. So, only one of you should go at a time."

Annie gulped and glanced at Jack. She stepped forward, her heart thumping. With slow, careful steps, she approached the unicorn. But as soon as it saw her, the unicorn took a step back, its eyes full of fear.

"Shhh... It's okay," Annie whispered, her voice gentle like a breeze. "It's okay... I won't hurt you. You're fine, and you're safe." She held out her hand, hoping the unicorn would trust her.

Annie did her best to maintain calm, but it didn't work. Rather than soothing the unicorn, it got super irate! The unicorn let out a loud, angry whinny and galloped deeper into the forest, disappearing among the trees.

Annie gave Jack a look, the kind of look that said everything without her even saying a word. Jack quickly understood what she meant: she had to follow the unicorn into the forest, no matter what.

Jack's face turned pale as he asked, "But what if the forest closes on you? You could get trapped in there indefinitely!"

Trying to stay brave, Annie took a deep breath and said, "If that happens, you need to keep shooting the spell. Please keep the way open for me, okay? Just keep doing it until I come out."

Jack nodded, though he didn't feel entirely convinced about this plan.

"But... how will we know if you're in trouble?" Jack questioned, his voice shaky.

Annie paused briefly, then quickly replied, "I'll send a message! It'll be ingrained in a red spark, and the spark will guide you right to me. Then, one of you can come assist me, okay?"

Before Jack could even answer, Annie turned and hurried into the forest after the unicorn, determined not to let it get away. Jack gazed at the trees, his heart pounding, hoping Annie would be safe there.

Panting hard, Annie ran through the dense forest, her heart pounding. Finally, she spotted the unicorn—cornered by a massive, black shadow! The unicorn's tail had already been torn off and tossed to the side. The shadow was closing in on the poor creature like it was about to gobble it up.

Annie had no second thoughts. She grabbed the tail, shoved it into her pocket, and yelled, "Hey! Leave it alone! Come on over here!"

The shadow froze, turning its snake-like head towards her. It wasn't like any monster Annie had ever seen, not even in her fairy-tale books. Her mind screamed one thing: Uh-oh! Now it's after me! RUN!

So, Annie ran like she was in the wildest marathon ever, with a tiger, bear, and lion all hunting her, their six hungry eyes locked on her legs as succulent steaks stapled to each one! "Eek!" she cried, shooting a red spark into the air with the image of the monster situation engraved inside it—just before the beast's sharp teeth sank into her leg!

It bit her! It felt like her leg was on fire, not like snake venom but like flames crawling up her skin. The pain was so bad she almost thought, I'd rather die if that makes it stop! But she knew she had to get away first. She raced around a corner, kicked a stone down the other path to make a loud noise, and tricked the monster into thinking she'd gone that way.

Breathing hard, she scrambled up to the nearest tree. Even if the monster figured out her trick, it wouldn't be able to reach her up here. Safe... for now.

Safe in the tree canopy, Annie finally looked at her leg. Blood was gushing out like a tiny fountain, and before she could think, her legs locked up! She tumbled right out of the tree, falling face-first into the mud! Worst part? Her mouth was wide open, so she swallowed some of that nasty mud, and some smeared onto her snakebite.

But guess what? That mud wasn't just gross—it was poisonous mud! It made her wound burn even more, and her body felt like it was spinning in circles like an anchor getting swung around and around. She felt so weak, as if her energy was being sucked right out of her.

Just then, the monster heard her fall and began heading toward her. Annie's heart sprinted, but she used her last bit of strength and swung herself back up into the tree. There, a bunch of branches twisted together like a hammock, making an excellent hiding spot. And because she and Jack had been smart enough to wear green and brown for their journey, she blended in like a ninja! The monster peered about but couldn't see her, hidden ideally in the leaves.

Annie felt strange, as if she were falling through an endless space, spinning into nothingness. Then, out of nowhere, a bright blue spark zipped through the leaves and stopped right before her. It wasn't just a spark, though—like magic, a flower was attached to it! Even though her vision was all fuzzy and she could barely see straight, she noticed something crazy: the spark had "Jack" carved right on it! So, it had to be from him!

The flower opened up like it was alive, and Annie squinted hard to read what it said...

Dear Annie,
I'm sorry I can't come! That monster you saw in your picture has started causing chaos. Everyone needs my help, and I can't just leave them! But don't worry; I've sent you the only flower to keep that monster's bite away.

Here's what you need to do:

1. Chew on the flower for thirty seconds.
2. Swallow it quickly.
3. Wait thirty seconds, and your wound will be all better!

I wish I could be there with you because I don't want you to do this alone! Please return as soon as possible if you have the unicorn's tail. We need you here! Just follow my instructions, and I promise you'll be okay.

Love,
Jack

Annie quickly stuffed the flower in her mouth, as if it were a super-magic snack that could save the world (and it was!). She chewed on it for thirty seconds, feeling like she was munching on something that tasted like cow manure, but she swallowed it like a champion! And wow, just like that, her strength returned-she felt like she could lift a thousand Herculeses all at once!

With a mighty shout, she leapt out of the treetops and raced back toward the forest's edge. Sure enough, the monster and Jack were fighting like they were in the world's craziest wrestling match, but the beast was winning! Jack looked distracted, and the forest started closing around them like it was trying to trap them forever.

Annie made a daring leap in time, flying over the treetops like a superhero before the trees snapped shut, taking the unicorn with them. But wait! Annie snatched a spiky branch from the ground before the forest clamped down. When the monster was busy trying to strangle Jack, she took off running as fast as her legs could go, jumped into the air, and swung that branch down with a BOOM!

It struck right onto the monster's head, breaking it into tiny pieces! Annie then pulled Jack out from under the dead monster's body with all her might, and just like that, all the yellow petals from the flowers vanished into thin air!

Annie rocketed over to another flower and yanked off its green petal. She read aloud: "SPIRITUAL: TEMPTATION TO RUN AWAY FROM DISTRESS." Just then, a giant bull demon sprang towards them, stomping and snorting like it meant business. But before she panicked, Annie remembered what the words meant and shouted to Jack, "We can't run away! We must stand our ground and trust the flowers won't hurt us!"

So, there they stayed, like two courageous statues, even though the tribals around them yelled, "Run! Turn back! Don't stay!" They had no idea Jack and Annie were standing there deliberately, trying to complete the challenge!

Right when the bull demon was about to smash them with its enormous horn, poof! It vanished into thin air, leaving only a swirl of glints behind. Just like that, all the green petals from the flowers vanished, too! Only three petals were left on each flower: a blue petal, an indigo petal, and a violet petal.

Jack didn't waste a second and dashed to the nearest flower to pluck the blue petals. He read the words aloud: "MAGICAL: COMBINE TWO SPELLS TO MAKE A SPELL THAT HAS THE QUALITIES OF BOTH THE PARENT SPELLS AND THE SPELL HAS TO BE SOMETHING NEVER DONE BEFORE."

Annie's eyes lit up. "I know! What if we mix an uproot spell with a create river spell? We could create a spell that can uproot rivers! That's never been done before!"

"Awesome idea!" Jack exclaimed. "Now, all we need is to ask the wish soil for a spell mixer, shoot the two spells inside, and mix until they're all swirly together!"

They high-fived, ready to tackle the next magical challenge!

Jack, Smoky, Smoky's family, and all the tribals cheered together, "Let's do it!"

Annie quickly squatted down and asked the wish soil for a spell mixer. When it popped up from the ground, all shiny and ready, she smiled and said to Jack, "Okay, I'll do the uproot spell, and you do the river spell. Ready? On the count of three... one... two... three!"

On three, Jack and Annie fired their spells into the spell mixer—zap! Zap!—and then slammed the lid shut faster than a cheetah on roller skates. Inside the mixer, the spells swirled around as glowing orbs of light—Annie's uproot spell was bright red, and Jack's river spell was shimmering blue. They cranked the handle like a game of super-fast ice cream churning, watching the lights roll and mix.

When they were done, a single purple orb of light floated out, glowing like the most incredible magic ever! It hovered for a second and then—whoosh!—zoomed straight into Jack's body.

Jack's eyes widened as he felt the magic fill him, as he'd just eaten the most potent, magical snack in the universe.

Jack waved at Annie, "All right, let's make a river we can uproot." They needed the river they crossed earlier to return home, but now they had to use their new magic trick.

Annie pointed her hands at the ground and cast a spell, and a river appeared out of nowhere, flowing smoothly over the patch of land.

Jack felt the new spell buzzing and aimed his hands at the river. He shouted, "Here goes nothing!" and fired the spell at it. Suddenly, the river shot out of the ground like a rocket, water flying everywhere, but instead of splashing down, it just hovered in the air, wrapped up in that glowing purple light.

Jack looked at Annie with wide eyes. "We just uprooted a river!"

Jack waved his hand, and the river followed, flowing in the air like a massive, magical serpent until he eventually directed it back into its spot in the ground. Just as the water level dropped, Annie cast a destruction spell, and the river vanished into thin air. Just like that, every single blue petal vanished from the flowers!

Without pausing for breath, Annie dashed to a flower and tugged its indigo petal. She read the message aloud, "TREASURE: GENERATE LIFE INTO THIS SEED." And then a tiny seed magically appeared in front of them, as if it had been dropped there by some invisible hand helping them out.

Jack blinked, scraping his head. "Annie, how in the world are we supposed to bring this seed to life? We're not God! How are we going to do this challenge?"

Annie's face suddenly lit up with an idea as bright as lightning. "I got it! We don't need to be gods. All we have to do is plant it in the soil!"

So, they asked the wish soil for gardening tools, live worms, compost, and a spray of their village's famous water. The moment the tools appeared, they jumped into action. They began by digging a small hole in the ground and carefully placing the seed inside. Next, they evenly distributed the compost over it and gently patted the soil down. They dropped the worms into their new home (with a little "eww!" from Jack) and eventually sprinkled the water over them.

And then, they waited.

It didn't take long. In just a few minutes, a new flower started to sprout, growing larger and larger until it had bloomed right before their eyes. It was stunning, but what stood out was the violet petal left on this new flower. In a flash, all the indigo petals disappeared from the other flowers, too, and they all looked just like the new one.

As soon as this challenge was over, Jack reached for the violet petal and plucked it. He read aloud: "MENTAL: OVERCOME YOUR GREATEST FEAR."

All of a sudden, everything went dark—like really dark. Dense shadows closed in around Jack, making it hard to see anything. He could barely hear his friends calling out to him. And then, deep in the darkness, he heard singing—a soft, eerie melody. Unconsciously, Jack began to pursue the sound. But then he heard a whisper in his ear, saying, "Never follow something you're unsure of. Try asking first."

Suddenly, vines shot out of nowhere and encased around Jack, holding him tight like a viper clutching its prey. A sweet smell filled the air, and soft, dreamy music crept into his ears. His eyelids became heavy, and his head drooped forward. He was fighting to stay awake, but then—WHAM! He got whacked in the head with a metal club! It felt like his head was on fire, burning like crazy. The music and the sweet smell suddenly became even more vital as someone cranked them up to maximum volume, and Jack couldn't tolerate it anymore. With a loud cry of pain, one that startled everyone else outside the darkness, Jack passed out cold.

All the flowers disappeared instantly, and two ice swords flew down from the sky, missing Annie by just a hair! Writing on them said, "You can keep these."

Then, all of a sudden, the darkness around Jack disappeared, and there he was, lying on the ground. Without wasting a second, Annie grabbed the ice swords and dashed to her brother, the tribals running close behind. When she reached him, she knelt, her heart racing. Fortunately for her, Jack's injuries weren't too severe. There was just a little bit of blood at the back of his head, but nothing super serious. He'd passed out from the pain, but Annie knew he'd wake up soon. Holding ice swords, she patiently waited for her brother to reopen his eyes.

Jack was still out cold, and someone had to stay with him to ensure he was okay. That's when a tribal lady named Lisa, who was super good with medicine, stepped up. She wrapped a bandage around Jack's head and took some gooey stuff made from tree sap and leaves. Then, she grabbed a strong piece of cloth and signalled two huge, bulky men to hold each end of it. Together, they lifted Jack onto the fabric like a stretcher and carried him along.

With Jack safely hoisted up, the group kept going. A few hours passed, and finally, Jack woke up, groaning but feeling way better. Even though awake, he stayed on the cloth until he was strong enough to walk with everyone again.

After hiking for some time, they finally reached the top of a mountain. But instead of a regular trail, there was a path made of clouds. Below it, though, was a massive, terrifying hole. If anyone took a wrong step and fell into it, that would be the end. It was pretty obvious: one mistake would spell disaster!

# 10.
# THE ENIGMA OF THE CLOUD PATH

They all froze, stopping so fast that Annie almost bumped into Wiseman. Jack looked at Wiseman and asked, "Wiseman, do you know where we are?"

Wiseman scratched his head. "Nope, I've never seen this place before," he said, looking just as puzzled as Jack felt.

Just then, Annie's eyes lit up like she had the best idea ever. "Jack, do you have the map in your bag?"

"Oh yeah!" Jack said. "Want me to get it out?"

"Yes, Jack, hurry!"

Jack started digging through his bag like a maniac, tossing out random stuff when his fingers brushed against something rough. He pulled it out and stared at it—it was the map! But it felt all weird and scratchy, which it definitely wasn't before. Jack was totally puzzled. He unfolded the map, looking for any clues, and just then, a red teardrop shape flipped upside down and appeared right over a bunch of tiny white blobs on the map.

"Hey, look!" Jack said, pointing at the map. "It says we're at the Cloud Path!"

Jack scratched his head, looking at the map, then back at the sky. "There's a problem, Annie. See, the map's path appears connected, but the clouds are all scattered here! We'd have to jump from one cloud to another, but they're far apart. If we miss, we might plummet down, which sounds like the worst way to end this adventure."

Annie's eyes narrowed like she was deep in thought. "Then there's only one option left, Jack."

Jack perked up. "What's that, Annie?"

"We'll have to figure out how to make these clouds stick together like a big, fluffy bridge. Then we can walk across safely." She turned to Wiseman, who was quietly watching them. "Wiseman, do you know how we could do that?"

They all stared at him, hoping he had some ancient trick up his sleeve.

Wiseman opened his mouth to answer, but then froze, a strange look on his face. He shivered a little, like he felt something spooky in the air. Jack noticed and whispered to Annie, "What's up with him?"

Wiseman finally spoke, his voice low and quiet. "I feel it—the same magic I felt when the witch attacked my village. The clouds aren't just clouds; they're made of magic. We'll have to wait for something… unusual to happen."

Jack and Annie glanced at each other as the group buzzed with guesses. "What kind of unusual thing?" someone asked. But just then—BOOM! Thunder boomed across the sky, and a massive flash of lightning lit the clouds. Everything went totally silent.

And then, out of nowhere, a soft voice spoke, like it was coming from the clouds themselves…

To some, a source of trust and love,
To others, a ball and a chain,
For me, some go beyond, above,
While others yet complain.
For I'm a thing you cannot choose,
You're stuck with what you've got,
Yet, I'm a thing that one can lose,

For granted, take me not.
The leaves, the branch, the roots, the seed,
The living crimson flow,
As each of them their lives, they lead,
Forever shall I grow.
What am I?

The whole army thought hard, looking totally puzzled by the riddle. They all tried to figure it out, but no one was sure what it meant. Jack suddenly had an idea and said, "Wait a minute... if the riddle is trying to tell us something, maybe we just need to focus on the simplest line and figure it out from there!"

He looked at everyone, his eyes bright with excitement. "And the simplest line is, 'To some, a source of trust and love!'"

Everyone leaned in, listening. "So, a source of trust and love... that must mean it's a group of people who really trust and care about each other!" Jack said, feeling like they were finally onto something.

Jack jumped up, fists in the air. "Yes!"

Annie's face lit up like she'd just cracked the code. "Jack's right! And the word for a group of people who trust and love each other is... family! Family's the answer!" She grabbed Jack's arm. "Since you figured it out, you should be the one to say it! Hurry, say it before we're stuck here forever!"

Jack leaned close to the cloud that had spoken the riddle, his voice barely a whisper. "Family."

For a second, nothing happened. Jack and Annie glanced at each other, worried they'd gotten it wrong. But then—BOOM! Thunder rumbled, lightning flashed, and rain poured down, drenching everyone until they were soaked. Just as fast as it started, it stopped. They all blinked, dry as if the rain never even happened.

As the sunlight dimmed just enough, they looked up and noticed the clouds were joined together, forming a solid path right in front of them!

They kept walking along the cloud path, not seeing much except the endless sky, a few eagles soaring above, and the land far below. Suddenly, they spotted a giant golden gate right in front of them! The gate made a strange noise and spoke in a robot-like voice, "To access entry, a riddle is on the other side of your map. It would be helpful if you could solve it. Good luck."

Jack and Annie blinked at each other, totally confused about the "good luck" part. But when they flipped the map over, everything fell into place. Right, there was a little screen, and on the screen was a picture, except it was all broken up into a bunch of small pieces scattered around the edges of an ample, empty grey space. It seemed to be waiting for someone to put the pieces back together.

Jack squinted at it, scratching his head. "Annie, what is this weird contraption? I feel like I've seen it before... back home."

"Maybe we should try to remember by stretching our brains," Jack suggested.

So, they "stretched" their brains as hard as possible, but still—nothing. Then it hit them: this was a puzzle! And if they didn't solve it, they might be stuck here forever. With a gulp, they swiped the pieces around the screen, trying to make sense of the scrambled picture.

They worked all night, swiping and moving pieces until their eyes got heavy, but they kept going. When they had only one piece left, morning sunlight peeked over the clouds, and the army woke up.

With a final swipe, they placed the last piece, and suddenly, the picture glowed and sank right through the screen. It floated over to the gate, touched it, and then vanished! The image showed Elsa holding a baby that looked just like her.

Then, without warning, the eight pillars around the gate started to spin faster and faster, shaking the whole cloud path under their feet!

# 11.
# SCULPTURES OF WONDER

Suddenly, the pillars started crumbling, and they turned into sculptures of fairies, shaking off bits of rock and showering tiny pebbles everywhere. Slowly, the fairies stretched out their wings, which looked super delicate, like one poke would snap them in half. But somehow, they seemed strong enough to help them fly! Jack and Annie stood there, staring at each other with mouths wide open.

Then, simultaneously, they blurted out, "Who are you, and why are you here, stuck inside pillars holding up a gate? Are you the legendary Fairies of the Elements? And is your leader 'The Bridge' between your world and ours, like in Elsa's tale?"

One fairy with shimmering golden wings stepped forward, totally calm and not even a little bit annoyed by all the questions. "Yes, we are the Fairies of the Elements," she said in a soft, steady voice, "and I am Elsa's daughter. My cousins here are Anna's daughters." She paused and looked at each of them. "We're here because a wicked witch kidnapped us in our sleep and trapped us here."

Jack and Annie gasped, hardly believing they were face-to-face with Elsa's daughter and the famous fairies of legend!

The fairy with the golden wings bared her teeth in a snarl. "You want to go to the witch's castle? Well, we'll come with you. We want revenge on that crooked, old witch who stole us away from our families. We also thank you for resolving all the challenges with the flowers. Right, sisters?"

The other fairies nodded in agreement, shouting a vast, united "YES!" The army stood there in shocked silence, not sure what to say.

Jack raised his hand, his brow furrowed in confusion. "Wait, if you're Elsa's daughter, then why do you have wings? Shouldn't you be... well, human?"

The fairy didn't seem upset at all. She just shrugged, unfazed. "Ah, well, that's a long story. My great-grandfather touched a fairy plant, and he got some fairy genes. I'm the first one to inherit those fairy genes since him. As for who he was... I have no idea. If I did, I would've told you sooner!"

Jack and Annie blinked, trying to take all this in. A fairy family with magical wings? This was becoming increasingly exciting!

Annie, always polite, smiled and asked, "Then, may we know your names and powers, please?"

One of the fairies with blue wings and a dress that sparkled like water stepped forward. She wore a delicate tiara made of shimmering droplets. "I'm Ripple," she said proudly. "I'm third in line to the throne and can control water."

Another fairy twirled forward, her dress of swirling violet smoke and her wings glowing a deep purple. "I'm Spirit," she said with a mysterious smile. "I'm fourth in line to the throne. I can manipulate objects with my thoughts, control the mind, and discover its mysteries."

Then, a fairy in a dress of golden sunbeams, with yellow wings like the first rays of morning, floated into view. She smiled warmly and radiantly, introducing herself as Moonlight. "I can control light, and I'm fifth in line for the throne."

A fiery fairy dressed in blazing flames and red wings stepped up. She was like a walking fire. "I'm Fume," she declared. "I'm sixth in line to the throne and can control fire."

A sixth fairy fluttered forward. She had a tiara and dress made of soft, swirling orange mist, and her wings were bright, glowing orange. She smiled breezily and introduced herself as Breeze. "I can control mist and air and am seventh in line for the throne."

Next, a fairy with an earthy look stepped up. Her dress was made of rich, brown soil and grass, and her wings were deep indigo. "I'm Pleasant," she said, her voice as calm as a gentle breeze. "I'm eighth in line to the throne and can control the earth."

A fairy with bright green wings and a crown of leaves appeared next. Her dress was a flowing mix of leaves, vines, and petals. "I'm Evergreen," she said proudly. "I'm ninth in line to the throne and can control plants."

Finally, the fairy who had been talking the most—the one with golden wings—spoke up again. She wore a dress and a crown, similar to Elsa's, with sparkling white veils and sleeves that shimmered in the light. "My name is Wonder," she said with grace. "I'm second in line to the throne. I can control ice, and I also share the powers of my six cousins. Ripple, for example, is my sister because ice is just a form of water." She paused, her smile bright. "I wear a crown because I'm the eldest, so you know." She winked as if this were important. "As you can see, we follow a fairy tradition where each of us has a name that matches our power. And one of the rules is that when a fairy child is told they're a fairy, their wings magically appear, and they can fly!"

Jack and Annie stood there wide-eyed as the fairies listed their extraordinary powers. Each one had a gift that seemed as magical as the next!

Annie's curiosity got the best of her, and she asked, "How are you and the flowers related?"

Wonder, the fairy with the crown, smiled slightly and answered, "Well, we each have our colour—except for me. Fume is awakened after the red petal, breeze after the orange, Moonlight after the yellow, Evergreen after the green, Ripple after the blue, Pleasant after the indigo, and Spirit after the violet. I was the last one to wake up, while all my sisters had already done so. I was the one who sent you the ice swords, remember?" She raised an eyebrow. "Does that answer your questions? Because we don't have time to waste asking more questions."

She gave them both a look that could freeze a dragon in its tracks—straight out of The Book of Scary and Glary Glares (which she might have read since it's an actual book). Jack mumbled, "Well, yeah, sort of."

"Well, then, let's get cracking! We have no time to lose," Wonder declared, her voice full of urgency.

As they were about to move, Wonder's sharp eyes spotted something. "Can I have a closer look at that frog?" she asked, pointing to Croaky sitting comfortably on Jack's shoulder.

"Oh, him?" Jack said, looking down at his little frog. "He's our pet, and his name is Croaky! Help yourself!"

Croaky gave a small croak, as if he were showing off, and Wonder leaned in for a better look.

Wonder gently cradled Croaky in her hands and whispered to him in soft, secret words. Jack and Annie could barely catch the words, as if they were meant only for the frog. Then, Wonder released him, and as soon as Croaky landed, a puff of thick smoke suddenly surrounded them. It was so dense, they couldn't see anything! When it finally cleared, they stared at their village head standing right before them!

Jack and Annie stood there, stunned, unsure if they were dreaming or going crazy. But before they could even blink, Jack suddenly blacked out from the shock! He would've fallen out of the clouds if Annie hadn't reacted so quickly. She grabbed him by the heels, pulled him back up through the clouds, and set him gently back onto the strong piece of cloth that had been carrying them all this time.

Wonder didn't seem to notice. She rushed to the village head, her face lighting up with joy. "Oh, darling, how I missed you!" she squealed, hugging him tightly.

Still checking on Jack (still knocked out cold), Annie blinked and asked, "Uh… what's going on here?"

Wonder turned to her with a bright smile. "He is my husband," she said, grinning, "and his name is Exaltor. We met in an enchanted field filled with pink and blue flowers. I convinced his parents to let us marry, and he became a prince when we did. Some of my fairy genes were passed on to him, and that's how he got the power to grow wings and change their colour whenever he liked. He's also a wizard—his family is descended from the sorcerer who enchanted your village! We had twins, and they got a mix of our powers. They can also gain the powers of my sister and cousins. We gave them to foster parents, good friends who met us in the village and kindly offered to take our children in and teach them."

Still staring at Exaltor and Wonder, Annie could hardly believe her ears. So much was happening at once, she couldn't keep up!

Wonder's eyes grew distant as she spoke, her voice soft but filled with emotion. "We said yes because, back then, there was almost no one we could trust. You see, Exaltor's grandmother... she's the same witch who trapped me and my cousins here. She's been causing chaos everywhere, wreaking havoc on everything we care about. Only we—my cousins and I—could stop her, but we couldn't look after our twins."

Annie listened carefully, wholly absorbed in the story.

Wonder's voice trembled a bit as she continued. "After the big battle with the witch, she kidnapped my cousins and me while Exaltor was severely hurt. We had to leave him behind for safety, but we swore we would return for him. We didn't want him to get caught up in the danger.

"When Exaltor recovered, he searched for me and my cousins day and night. He never gave up, even though he never found us. Eventually, he had no choice but to settle down and care for the village, knowing we would be reunited one day when the time was right. But he never stopped hoping. And then, when he found out that two twins were going after the witch's treasure, he knew he couldn't let them face the danger alone. He had to protect them. He knew they'd need him."

Annie exchanged a look with Wiseman, realizing just how much Exaltor had been through, how much he'd sacrificed. Everybody couldn't help but feel a little in awe of him.

As they approached the gate, the fairies fluttered behind them, ready to help. Annie couldn't hold it in anymore and turned to Exaltor. "Is what Wonder said true? Are your twins safe? And where are the foster parents? What were their names?"

Exaltor smiled kindly at her and nodded. "Of course, it's true. It's in Wonder's family, not to lie. Our twins were safe, and Bill and Mary were the ones who took care of them. They raised them with all the love they could give."

Annie's eyes went wide, and her mouth dropped open. She stuttered in complete shock, "B-b-but th-that m-m-means you t-t-two are our p-p-parents! And...and..." she stopped stuttering and stood up straighter, her voice more confident now, "...that means Jack and I are royalty! We're part wizard and witch, part fairy, and we have Elsa's powers, too! Right? Right?"

Wonder looked at Exaltor with wide eyes, trying to ensure she heard him right. "Is it true, sweetie? Are they the twins we named Annie and Jack?"

Exaltor smiled warmly and nodded. "Yes, love. I remember it as if it were yesterday, even during a stormy night. We gave them to Bill and Mary, and I've been watching over them ever since. And Annie... she's the treasure I asked you to find. You've found her."

As soon as he said that, something amazing happened! Annie gasped as she felt a tingle in her back. She turned around to see shiny gold wings sprouting from her shoulder blades. She couldn't believe it! She flapped them and, whoosh! She was soaring through the air, flying like a bird for the first time. Her wings sparkled and glowed in the sunlight, and she giggled excitedly.

But then, she glanced down at Jack. He was still lying there, completely unconscious, as if the shock had knocked him out cold. "Jack, wake up!" Annie called, but it was no use—he wasn't stirring.

# 12.
# HEXED AND TAKEN

As Annie figured out she could fly, a wave of exhilaration washed over her. At first, she wobbled and spun forward, almost crashing right down through the clouds, but then—whoosh!—she managed to steady herself and zoom up, up, up into the sky. Her heart thumped as she did three huge loop-the-loops, her whoops echoing through the clouds like a needle.

Then, she shot up super high and let herself drop through the clouds, over and over, giggling down like she was on the best roller coaster ever. Then—out of nowhere—she shrank herself! She squealed again, and this time, it came out as a squeaky little mouse voice, which made her laugh so hard that she almost shrank even smaller. When she got big again, her shout was scratchy, like a frog. Finally, she made herself normal-sized and hovered right above Wonder and Exaltor's heads, feeling like the coolest kid ever.

With her eyebrows raised high and a big grin, Annie called down, "Hey, why am I flying already while Jack is still blacked out on that stretcher? And, uh, why are my wings all shiny gold?"

Wonder gave Annie a warm, reassuring smile and said, "There's one huge thing you're forgetting, my dear. When a fairy child is finally told they're a fairy, that's the moment their wings start growing. It's the most important rule of fairy tradition! And here's another cool part—fairies can hide their wings in their backs whenever they don't need them. And your wing colour? It reveals a great deal about who you truly are.

"For example, black wings mean a fairy is 100 per cent set on causing trouble and using their powers for all the wrong things. Some fairies even get so scared of this that they dye their kids' wings golden, thinking it'll make them good, but the colour doesn't change who they are inside! You, however? Like mine, your wings are golden all on their own, which means you're destined to be a good fairy with a heart of gold."

Just then, Spirit piped up, "My wings are purple, which shows I'm open-minded. Moonlight's wings are yellow—she's super trustworthy. Fume's wings are red, which means she's got a fiery personality. Ripple has blue wings because she's mostly calm. Breeze's wings are orange, which matches her gentle nature. Pleasant's wings are indigo since she's super patient. And Evergreen's green wings make her aura all mystical and nature-like."

Wonder smiled and said, "Your wings can only be one of these eight colours, but if you have more than one special trait, the strongest one will show in your wings. Got any other questions, my little one?"

Annie nodded, eyes wide with curiosity. "Yeah, just one more! What colour will Jack's wings be?"

Wonder laughed softly. "I can't answer that, sweetie—I don't know."

With a mother's love shining in her eyes, Wonder gently lifted Annie's face toward the light and pulled her into a warm hug. "You were just a month old when your father and I left you with Bill and Mary. You two were so peaceful, snoozing away in your little basket, unaware of the world around you. And now, seeing you so grown-up, it feels like that stormy night swept in just yesterday, and we left you on that doorstep. You two slept through the whole storm without a single peep!"

"I can't believe Jack and I have been living a HUGE, GIANT, ENORMOUS lie our whole lives! Why did you leave us like that? Leave us on a doorstep?" Annie asked, her voice all wobbly and hurt.

Wonder knelt and cupped Annie's face in her hands. "To protect you," she said softly. "If we'd taken you into battle, you wouldn't have made it."

Annie took a shaky breath and threw her arms around her mother, hugging her as if she'd never let go again. It felt as if she did, her mom might vanish into thin air! After a long moment, Annie finally looked up and noticed something ahead—where the path ended, the mountain sloped down toward a dark, creepy tunnel, leading right into another huge mountain.

They walked closer. Jack had woken up by now, and he was looking at the tunnel, too. Right at the entrance to the tunnel was a crooked old sign that read in all capital letters:

## THE EYEBALL TUNNEL

Just then, Annie's eyes went wide because this MASSIVE boulder shaped into a door was in front of them. But not just any door. Oh no. This one was twisted and weird-looking, like it had been carved by someone who loved making things look terrifying. And then, the door SPOKE.

Yep, you heard that right.

In this long, low, hissing voice, like a giant snake that had somehow learned English, the door said, "Helloooooooo, travelerrrrrrssssssssss…"

Annie gasped, and the whole army jumped back. This was one of the witch's obstacles, no doubt about it!

"My one-hundredth visitorsssssssssss!" the creepy door continued, stretching out each word like it was casting a spell. "If yoooooooouuuuuu can make it throoooooough me withouuuuuut dyyyyyyyyyying froooooom the tooooooooouch oooof myyyyyyyy aciiiiiiiiiiiiiid eyeballssssssss, overrrrrrrrrrr whichhhhhhh yoooooooooouuuuuu havvvvvve toooooo jummmmmmmp, I givvvvve yoooooooouuuu myyyyyy word that I willllllll open up anotherrrr doorrrrrrrr forrrrr yoooooooouuuuuuu, and if I doooo noooooooot keeep myyyy proooooomissssse, yoooooouuuuuu can make meeeeee tuuuurn intoooooo dust and rubbbbbble looong fooorgooootten FOREVERRRRRRRR!"

The whole place went still as the voice went on. "I willllllll sennnnnnnnnnd a huuundreeeeeed eyyyebaaaallllls becausssse I havvvvve ooonlyyyyyyy a huuundreeeeed eyeeees to roooooooollllll atttt yooouuuu annnnnd the nuuuuumberrrrrr wiiiiiiiiillll get noooo lessssserrrrrrr!"

Then, the door added one last challenge. "Nooooow I shaaaaaall oooooopen my doooooor foooooor yoooooouuuu toooo maaaaaaybeee esssscape out the otherrrrrrrrrrrrrr side oooorrrrr noooooot. MWA-HA-HA-HA-HA-HA-HA-HA!"

With a slow, rumbling creak and a resounding, hollow clunk, the giant door creaked open, revealing nothing but blackness so dark it looked like it might swallow them whole. They all took a deep breath, gathered their courage, and stepped in.

As soon as they did, torches flickered to life along the walls, casting a spooky, flickering glow around them. Jack (who STILL didn't have his wings yet, by the way) took a quick look around, thinking fast.

"Maybe we should tell everyone to line up in rows," he whispered to Annie, glancing around. "That way, we can move faster and keep the sides open, just in case we have to dodge those acid eyeballs."

Everyone gulped, readying themselves as they looked at each other, hearts thumping, ready for whatever came next!

"That's actually a pretty good idea!" Exaltor boomed, glancing around. "Let's put it to a vote. Hands up if you think Jack's idea rocks!"

Everyone's hands shot up like rockets. "Then it's settled!" Wonder said with a nod.

Exaltor turned to the whole army and shouted, "Alright, everybody! Spread out, ten people per line. Fairies and Wiseman, you lead the front!" He took a deep breath before giving his big warning. "Get ready to jump over any rolling eyeballs! If any part of you touches an acid eyeball, it'll burn up right then and there! You might end up missing an arm or leg by the time we're out of this smelly, nasty tunnel. So jump, then run straight until you see another eyeball! If you see too many eyeballs coming at you, just dodge—don't even try to jump!"

Everyone was just about to start moving when one of the eyeballs rolled right up to them, and guess what? They realized the creepy voice had totally lied! Some of these eyeballs were actually on fire instead of covered in acid.

Smoky, who'd been super quiet this whole time just listening to Annie, Wonder, and Exaltor, suddenly yelled to everyone, "Listen up, change of plan! If there's a flaming eyeball in your way, get out of there fast! If it's not on fire, jump over it! And if a whole bunch of them are coming at once, dodge!"

And just like that, everyone was off, jumping, dodging, and running. But then—pants started catching fire! People yanked them off as fast as possible and chucked them aside. The pants were toast, literally.

Flying up above the chaos, Jack, Annie, Wonder, Smoky, his family, Exaltor, and the fairies looked down. Jack was being carried by Smoky, as he had not yet got his wings. They knew they had to help, so they cast spells like crazy to keep everyone safe. Some spells made people float just enough to keep their legs from touching the burning eyeballs. Others put magical shields around people who'd already lost their pants to the fire and acid.

By working together, everyone managed to get through it. They weren't just a bunch of people now—they were like a vast team, looking out for each other through all the chaos.

Everyone made it safely to the other side of the tunnel—but not without a close call! Just as the last of the flaming and acid eyeballs came rolling all at once, the people flying near the tunnel's ceiling started freaking out.

"They're in big trouble! How can we help all of them? We can't carry everyone!" Evergreen shouted, looking down in panic.

Annie's eyes lit up. "Wait! We could try the flying spell on everyone! I really hope it works!"

"Let's do it!" Everyone cheered at the same time.

So, without a second thought, they all started casting the flying spell repeatedly until every person in the army was floating up to the ceiling. Then, like one huge flock of magical people, they all flew together toward the other side of the tunnel. Right on time, too, because just as they reached the end, the big stone door creaked open like the tunnel had promised. Together, they soared out, free and safe—at least for now!

Finally, they were out of the tunnel, all safe and sound. But after all this running, dodging and panicking, everyone was starving. When they checked their satchels, they found that every bit of food was gone! Not even a single crumb left.

People started to freak out, but Wonder and Exaltor, totally calm and relaxed, spoke up in perfect unison, "Everyone, don't worry! Just think of the meal you want, and it'll appear right in front of you."

Everyone gave it a try—Jack, Annie, Smoky, his family, Wonder, Exaltor, everyone! And poof! A giant, magical table appeared before their eyes, stretched as long as a dragon and full of food! Half the table was loaded with their tribe's most exceptional, celebratory dishes because they'd just made it through the eyeball tunnel of doom!

On the other side of the table was the most awesome spread of candy fruits from Sleepyfield! There were giant baskets of japples (juicy apples with jelly inside!), big bowls of manchocos (liquid-chocolate-filled mangoes!), heaps of tuavas (toffee-stuffed guavas!), and—get this—super-sweet gackfruits! These gackfruits weren't just any gackfruits; inside each one were edible gems. Rubies had mousse inside, and emeralds had truffle, both of which were chocolate-flavoured. It was like a fruit explosion of dessert dreams.

Everyone dug in, chomping and munching until they were so full they could burst. Just as they finished their epic meal, a huge clap of thunder boomed, followed by a voice so loud and mean it made everyone's ears ache.

"You weaklings!" it roared, "Weaklings, I say! Go back to your tiny, dung-filled village if you know what's good for you! Or else, you'll run into a nasty surprise, break down in sorrow, and I'll finish you off for all eternity while you're weeping in regret!"

Exaltor and Wonder both touched their throats with glowing fingers, whispering, "Akramant!" Suddenly, Exaltor's voice boomed even louder than that awful, thunderous one above, "You will NEVER win this war, Grandmother Polliexa! We have power over you—power you'll never have, no matter how hard you try!"

Wonder jumped in, her voice somehow even louder, ringing out like a battle trumpet, "Let us take what we came for if you're wise or face a defeat that will last forever! And instead of you finishing us, it'll be us finishing YOU!"

Their voices echoed through the sky, shaking the ground, and for a second, Polliexa's nasty voice was utterly silent.

The voice cackled, all sneery and mean, "Oh, is that so? Well then, I'll just take half of your power and hide it somewhere you'll never find it!"

Exaltor stood tall and laughed right back, "Oh really, Grandmother Polliexa? And how exactly do you think you're going to pull that off? I think that last battle made you a bit too confident. But this time, it's different!"

Polliexa's voice hissed back, "I'll make it happen by capturing your very best fighters and locking them away in my own fortress! Then we'll see how much your army can really do when they're locked in a place only I have the key to! None of your precious fighters will escape me! MWA-HA-HA-HA-HA-HA-HA-HA-HA-HA-HA-HA-HA-HA!"

Her laugh echoed and echoed, bouncing off every rock, getting louder until it felt like the whole world was filled with her creepy, wicked laugh.

Just as Polliexa's voice cut off, a gigantic lightning bolt cracked the sky open, and suddenly, thick, creepy smoke started swirling everywhere, turning everything into a dark, spooky fog. Out of nowhere, nine giant tentacles made of storm clouds whipped down like monster snakes, wrapping around people super-fast! Nobody even had time to yell "Help!" before the tentacles yanked them up with a whoosh, and their screams echoed through the foggy air as they were snatched away, disappearing right into the smoky sky.

Then, a heartbeat later, the ground started shaking like a million elephants were doing jumping jacks! People were flung everywhere like they had been tossed in a salad. Finally, when the earthquake calmed, everyone except Lisa, Wiseman, Smoky, and Smoky's family were sprawled out on the soft grass, totally out cold from bonking their heads on rocks or each other!

# 13.
# CLOAKED IN DARKNESS

Back at the creepy, dark castle, the stormy tentacles suddenly appeared, dropping the knocked-out hostages onto the cold stone floor with a thud. Then, they grabbed this gigantic jug filled with some gross-looking brown liquid and took a tiny tablet from a box labelled:

ANAESTHETIC TABLETS

MORE THAN 8 HOURS COMPLETE KNOCKOUT IF YOU TAKE THE WHOLE BOX

ONE TABLET – ONE HOUR

RECOMMENDED BY: POLLIEXA

They plopped the tablet into the jug and then added a single drop of something from a bottle on a nearby shelf that said:

KNOCKOUT LIQUID

1 DROP FOR ONE HOUR

TOO MUCH CAN CAUSE INSTANT DEATH

RECOMMENDED BY: POLLIEXA

Mixing it up with a creepy metal spoon, the liquid turned a weird shade of pink, and they spooned some into the hostages' mouths to ensure they stayed asleep for at least two hours. Then, the tentacles put themselves on guard, ready for Polliexa.

A few minutes later, Polliexa waltzed in, dressed like the ultimate Evil Queen. Her ankle-length, silky black gown trailed behind her, glittering with gems along the bottom and on her cape. She wore towering black heels, dramatic black makeup, sleek gloves, shiny bracelets, and a crown made of rare black-swan gold, shimmering with diamonds, sapphires, rubies, and all sorts of stolen jewels from Exaltor's village (yep, she still had them after winning that battle seven years ago!).

With a wicked grin, she whispered, "Finally! My tentacles have captured my sneaky grandson and my dear relatives. Did you give them the special sleepy drink?"

The tentacles wiggled around like they understood every word and gave a nod to Polliexa's question. She let out a wild cackle, "Yes! The time is finally here to regain my powers with a little help from my evil buddy, Wanda! Now, tentacles, listen up—keep the prisoners comfy, give them anything they want except freedom, right? I'll be waiting here until they wake up. Oh, speaking of that, how long will they be out?"

One of the tentacles floated close and whispered some total gibberish into her ear. She screeched, "Two hours? That's forever! Change it to thirty minutes right now! I can't wait to see their faces when they realize they're in my castle! Hee-hee-hee-hee-hee!"

Then, nine of the tentacles grabbed metal spoons and held them over each prisoner's mouth. Slowly, a sparkly, golden mist started rising from the hostages' lips and gathered in the spoons, like magical juice or something. The tentacles carefully poured all that golden mist into a bowl that the tenth tentacle had been holding the whole time. As soon as the last sparkle hit the bowl, it transformed into a strange, yellow liquid with brown streaks swirling through it. Then, they tossed the weird mixture out the window as if it were nothing.

After the tentacles shortened the sleeping time to thirty minutes, Polliexa snapped her fingers, making a fancy chair with an ottoman appear beside her and a giant spell book resting on top. She plopped into the chair, got comfortable, and said, "All right, tentacles—outside the door, on guard duty, now!" And with that, she began flipping through her book, ready to spring her next evil plan into action.

# 14.
# VERBAL FURY AND THE PORTAL'S PULL

In Polliexa's castle, the clock was ticking—twenty-nine out of thirty minutes had zipped by, and Polliexa's "hostages" were starting to wake up. Polliexa noticed this right away, snapping her spellbook shut and sitting up, her evil grin getting wider by the second. Just then, Wonder and Exaltor both gave a huge sneeze—ACHOO!—and, believe it or not, a golden sparkle flew right out of their ears! The sneeze was so strong it made them sit straight up, wide-eyed.

Wonder rubbed her eyes, looking around all groggy and confused. She squinted into the dim light, then mumbled, like she was talking to herself, "Where…where am I? What is this place? And how did I even get here?"

Polliexa smirked, her face practically glowing with evil pride. "Not-so-dear granddaughter-in-law and sneaky grandson," she sneered, "You're in The Black Castle, my very own castle that I built for me because your grandfather"—she shot a pointed finger at Exaltor—"wouldn't let me stay in your village after I used black magic to give me and my best friend, Wanda, long lives! He thought I'd cause trouble just because I wanted to stay in your so-called 'precious' village."

Her voice turned even sharper. "You should feel ashamed, you absolute fools! All you care about are people who aren't even related to you! I wanted revenge for kicking me out, and I got it! I caused all sorts of chaos to settle there when I couldn't before. And guess who messed up my plans? HIM!" She pointed at Exaltor with such force that you'd think she was trying to stab him with her finger. "Your grandfather defeated me, just like he destroyed every other plan I ever had! Seven years ago, I was this close to getting my revenge, but no, I couldn't finish you off. So, what did I do? I brought you here thinking this time would be different. And guess what? For the first time, I actually succeeded in part of my plan!"

Polliexa paced back and forth with excitement, not stopping for breath. "So, you can thank your grandfather for all this. If he'd just let me stay in your village after Wanda and I used black magic, you wouldn't be stuck here. We could've all lived together like a nice, happy family! But nooo, now you're mine!" She gave a wicked laugh, her eyes sparkling with triumph.

Polliexa's long, drawn-out speech finished with a sharp, nasty tone like she was about to burst into flames. But that smile on her face? It was all sarcasm and evil. Wonder didn't blink or flinch, though. She just took a moment to think about what Polliexa said, and then she snapped back.

"Well, first of all, why did you even use black magic in the first place?" Wonder's voice was calm, but a storm of anger was brewing in her eyes. "Everybody has to die eventually! You didn't explain that, did you? And you didn't explain why you were so rude to us that I'm this close to just blowing up in fury! You've got everything wrong, Polliexa. Everything."

Polliexa's face twisted into a frown, but Wonder didn't care. "See, here's the truth. He did think you'd cause chaos. You can't blame him for that, especially since Wanda and your black magic turned you into this… this thing you are now. You don't even see it, do you?" Wonder's voice rose with each word, her frustration pouring out like a waterfall. "You're not you anymore. Wanda's been using you the whole time, and you're too blind to see it. She made you think that black magic would make you stronger, but really? She's just twisting you up inside."

Wonder pointed right at Polliexa, her finger trembling with the weight of her words. "She convinced you to use the magic for your benefit, but it's all been about her getting what she wants—not you. You've been corrupted, Polliexa, and you don't even know it."

Polliexa's eyes widened, and she screamed at Wonder, her voice shaking with fury, "LIES! All of it lies! Filthy, outrageous, complete lies!"

Wonder wasn't phased. She just shook her head slowly, her voice dropping into something profound and full of concern. "You think Wanda was your best friend, huh? Well, listen up, Polliexa. A true friend who cares about you wouldn't encourage you to do evil things. She would've tried to stop you, not help you! Wanda isn't your friend. She's been using you the whole time. She wants your power, too, after you've ruined the village and taken all our powers, and then, she plans to rule the world with all the magic she can control. Think about it—she doesn't care about you."

Wonder took a deep breath and continued, now sounding more worried than angry. "We're your family, Polliexa. We care about you! We don't want anything bad to happen to you, especially not now. You could" She paused, looking around at the others, then whispered, "You could go any minute. You don't even know how close you are."

She stared at Polliexa, her voice soft but firm. "So, dear grandmother-in-law, I think you've got the whole story all wrong. It's a huge misunderstanding, and I'm telling you now before it's too late."

Right as Wonder finished, Exaltor began preparing a truthful speech in his mind. Since he woke up, he had been silently connecting with Annie and Jack through telepathy. The magic had let them hear the whole argument, and Exaltor knew it was time to act. He needed to calm his grandmother down before things got out of control.

Telepathy wasn't easy. Only wizards with real experience could use it without falling into a trance, but Exaltor was one of the best. He could communicate without losing focus. So, he reached out to Annie and Jack, showing them the heated argument and preparing for the next step. He was about to step in, hoping he could help stop Polliexa before she completely lost it.

Exaltor took a deep breath, his voice calm but full of urgency. "Please, dear grandmother, listen to me. Let me tell you a secret," he said, his eyes softening. "Wonder isn't just anyone. She comes from a royal family, a family with a big tradition. When royal family members turn eight, they have to make a vow. A vow that they will never lie for their entire life. And if they do, they'll be cursed and banished from the royal palace forever.

Wonder took that vow, and she's kept it. It's in her blood. She can't lie, not even if she wanted to. Every word she has said to you and everything she told you is the truth. Whether you believe her or not, the truth will always be the same."

Exaltor finished speaking, his voice dropping into a mix of frustration and shame. He hated having to say it, but it was the truth. He looked at Polliexa, hoping she would finally understand.

At that exact moment, Fume let out a huge sneeze. She jumped up from its force, her body rocketing so high that she hit the ceiling! The room went silent for a second as everyone stared at her in surprise.

Fume suddenly toppled over, her nose bleeding as she hit the floor with a thud. She blinked a few times, rubbed her eyes, and then looked around like she was trying to figure out where she was. Slowly, she pushed herself up, groaning a bit, and turned to Wonder, asking, "Ouch! That really hurt! Royal Sister? Could someone tell me what we are doing in this super dark and gloomy castle?"

Wonder quickly answered, "Fume, I trust you remember Polliexa from our last battle... the one where we, um, got totally defeated."

Fume squinted at Polliexa, eyes widening as she noticed something strange. "Wait... is she really our opponent?! But she looks so... young!

How can she be the same bent, warty, old Polliexa we fought before? I mean, no offence to Polliexa, but there's no way anyone would think she's the same person! She looks way too young for all this war stuff! She doesn't even look like she could lift a knife against a fly!"

Polliexa scowled, her face turning red with irritation. "Hey! All I have to do is wait for Wanda to show up, and then I'll be more powerful than all of you put together!" She crossed her arms, looking like she was trying to act tough, but her voice was full of annoyance.

Back at the tribal camp, Annie and Jack started to slowly wake up, their eyelids fluttering as they stirred from unconsciousness. Meanwhile, Smoky noticed them moving and rushed over to them.

Smoky, his voice full of hope and concern, said, "Come on, you two. You can do it. Please come back to us."

# 15.
# EXPLORING CELESTIUM: THE POWER OF SEVEN

A little while later, Jack's body was lying on a cloth on the ship, and out of nowhere, golden wings sprouted from his back! They shimmered in the sunlight, big and majestic, like something straight out of a fairy tale.

*Meanwhile, in Annie's Celestium…*

I woke up feeling all soft and floaty, as if I were lying on a giant marshmallow. The sky above me was a swirl of pink and purple, like cotton candy mixed with the most beautiful sunset. But the weird thing was, the sky didn't stretch on forever. It only went as far as where I was, and below that, it was all dark and mysterious.

For a second, everything went totally black, and it felt like I was zooming down a super steep slide, my stomach dropping! But then, the blackness disappeared, and I was in this strange purplish-pink sky. I was flung up into the air and landed softly on a cloud that felt like the fluffiest pillow. Everything felt... off, though. How did I even get here? Was I stuck? And wait—why did everything feel so familiar?

I tried to shake the feeling and called out, "Hello? Is anybody there?"

Suddenly, I heard a voice from way off in the distance. "Annie, is that you?"

I recognized that voice instantly—Jack! I tried to paddle through the air, but whoa—I lost my balance and fell off my cloud.

When I finally dared to unscrew my eyes open (because I had squeezed them shut in fear before), I found myself on yet another pink-purplish cloud. This one was as soft and fluffy as the last, like I was floating on a giant cotton candy. I couldn't help but wonder if another cloud had moved to catch me when I fell, sensing my fear. But I knew that couldn't be true.

Still, I figured, why not give it a try? I focused hard, willing the clouds to form a path to Jack's cloud. And in less than a minute, poof! A trail of clouds stretched out before me, leading to a cloud far off in the distance.

Excited, I skipped and hopped across the clouds. It felt like I had total control over them—I was the one making them do what I wanted! It was amazing!

But when I finally reached Jack's cloud, my heart sank. Jack wasn't there. The cloud was empty, like he had never been there at all.

Before I could think about it too much, a voice I knew all too well echoed through the air. "Hello, daughter. You must be wondering where Jack has gone."

I spun around quickly, my heart racing, and saw a face made entirely of clouds, shaped just like Exaltor's face. I was about to say something, but before I could, Exaltor's voice came urgently, "There's no time to talk. I have to show you where we are and what's going on so you can help us."

Suddenly, his cloud face split open, and it turned into a very old lady's face. She was covered in dark black makeup, and her expression was creepy, like something straight out of a nightmare. "This," Exaltor said, his voice serious, "is your great-grandmother, the witch. She's guarding the treasure that you and Jack are after. She kidnapped us with her tentacles because she and her friend want to steal our village and powers."

As soon as he said that, a loud, chaotic argument erupted in front of me—Wonder, Exaltor, and my great-grandmother were yelling at each other, their words mixed up in a blur. It was like a scene from a play, but it was all happening right in front of me.

After the fight ended, Exaltor's cloud face calmed down, his voice soft but firm. "I'm going to make your brother visible now," he said. "Your Celestium is a place where you can think, work, and learn without hurting the world outside. It's like a secret lab inside your mind where you can practice magic or do anything without needing food, water, sleep, or air. I'm going to help extend your magic powers, your aunts' and your mother's, too, until there's nothing more to learn. It might take days, but time doesn't work the same here."

I blinked. It sounded strange, but if anyone could do it, it was Exaltor. And if it meant helping save our village and family, then I was ready.

"Imagine all the amazing things you could do with these powers," Exaltor said, his voice full of excitement.

I couldn't help but think about it. My mind spun with the possibilities—new heights, new abilities, endless adventures!

But before I could get lost in those thoughts, something strange happened. The cloud I was standing on felt different. It wasn't empty anymore—it was like I had run into an invisible wall. I blinked, and the wall slowly started to fade away, like mist in the morning. And then, I saw him. Jack.

His figure grew clearer and clearer, as if someone were drawing him back into the world. And before I knew it, we were wrapped in a big, warm bear hug! It felt incredibly comforting, as if everything would be okay.

Grinning, I pulled back a little and asked, "So, Jack, how does it feel to be inside a Celestium?"

Jack blinked, looking around, confused. "Celestium? What's that?"

I smiled and swept my arms out, gesturing to the swirling, magical space around us. "This!" I said, feeling a little proud of myself. "This is the Celestium! I guess you weren't listening to Exaltor. It's like a place where you can believe and practice whatever you want without hurting the world outside. It's like... a secret training ground for magic! Please listen carefully to what Exaltor says next time."

Jack's eyes widened. "Whoa, that's cool! But I was busy looking around, so I couldn't hear him. "

"Never mind."

After explaining what the Celestium was, I felt like Jack was finally starting to get the hang of it. Jack said, "ok. I understood everything except... why do you have wings?"

I took a deep breath and said, "Okay, so Wonder and Exaltor—they're our real parents, and that makes us half-fairies. That's why I have wings."

As soon as the words left my mouth, Jack's eyes went wide. And before I could blink, golden wings popped out of his back! They looked just like mine—shiny, shimmering, and gleaming with that golden glimmer. He gasped and started flying around, zooming and spiralling through the air like a little whirlwind.

"Whoa!" Jack cried, twisting around in mid-air, staring at his wings. "These are... real! How did this happen?"

I watched him fly all over the place, weaving in and out of the soft clouds like a playful butterfly. He looked so surprised and excited at the same time. But then he stopped, hovering above me, and looked kind of worried.

"I don't want golden wings! I like blue wings!" he said, frowning. "Blue's my favourite colour, not gold!"

I giggled a little and floated up to him. "You can't choose the colour of your wings, Jack. It's not how it works. Your wings are golden because, deep down, there's something in you that matches the colour gold. It's a trait that's inside you, even if you don't know it. If you had a trait that matched blue, then you would've gotten blue wings. But gold is what you got, and that's pretty special."

Jack blinked and looked at his wings again, still unsure. "Hmm, I guess golden's not so bad." He tried out a few more twirls, this time with a bit more confidence. "Maybe gold wings aren't so bad after all."

Jack stopped flying around and hovered next to me, his golden wings sparkling in the soft light of the Celestium. He looked at me with a curious frown. "I'm wondering… how did you get wings before me?"

I thought about it for a second, then smiled. "Well, I was told that I'm a half-fairy first. If you're told you're a half-fairy, that's when your wings will grow. So, I guess I got them first because I learned about it earlier."

Right then, Exaltor's cloud face appeared above us. It was all misty and floating like something out of a dream. He nodded at Jack, then me, and said, "Now it's time for you two to unlock your magic."

I blinked, trying to focus. "What do we do?"

"Lie down, and start visualizing your magic washing over you," Exaltor explained. "Feel it, like it's moving through you. When the process is complete, you'll feel like you're wet, but you won't actually be wet. It's a special kind of magic."

I nodded and lay back on the soft cloud, closing my eyes. Jack did the same. I imagined a wave of shimmering magic flowing through my body, from my head to my toes. It felt warm and powerful but also soft, like a gentle stream. I felt something tingle in my fingers and then my toes, as if my whole body was waking up.

I didn't feel wet when I finished the visualization, but I could tell something had changed. Exaltor's cloud face nodded in approval. "Good. Now, you must meditate on your chakras. Sit up cross-legged and focus on your breathing. The magic you just felt will speed up the process. It'll only take a few minutes, but you must concentrate."

I sat on my cloud, crossed my legs, and breathed slowly. In. Out. In. Out. The air felt fresh, and everything around me seemed to calm down.

Exaltor's voice echoed softly in the Celestium, guiding us as we sat on my cloud, ready to unlock our magic. "Okay, you two, let's begin. Visualize a rich, red light at the bottom of your spine. This is your root chakra, the Muladhara. Take a deep breath, and imagine roots growing from your body deep into the earth, like a giant tree. Feel the earth below you, solid and strong. Picture any blocked energy melting away, and let yourself feel safe, grounded like you're part of the earth."

I closed my eyes, took a deep breath, and imagined that red light glowing warmly. Slowly, I pictured big roots sprouting from my spine, digging deep into the ground. It felt like I was a tree, sturdy and calm.

"Good," Exaltor's voice said. "Now, picture an orange light in your lower belly. This is your sacral chakra, the Svadhisthana. Breathe deeply into this space, and imagine water flowing freely through you. Feel the flow, like a calm river, gentle but strong."

I focused on the orange light. I could feel the water inside me, calm and flowing. It felt peaceful, like a river without obstacles.

"Next," Exaltor continued, "think about a bright yellow light in your solar plexus area. This is your solar plexus chakra, the Manipura. Make the light grow brighter with each breath, fuelling your inner fire. Let it fill you with energy, like the sun powering you from the inside."

I pictured a glowing yellow light in the centre of my stomach. With each breath, it grew brighter, like the sun lighting up my whole body. I could feel it giving me energy, making me feel strong.

"Now, focus on a soft green light in your chest. This is your heart chakra, the Anahata. Breathe deeply and let this light expand, filling you with love, kindness, and compassion. Feel the warmth grow as your heart opens."

I felt the green light spreading through my chest, making me feel warm and peaceful. It was like the light was hugging me, filling me with love.

"Next, picture a blue light at your throat. This is your throat chakra, the Vishuddha. Breathe deeply, and imagine this blue light clearing away any blockages, letting you speak your truth and be heard."

The blue light was calm and calming. I imagined it washing away anything that made it hard to speak, like a wave washing away the sand.

"Now, focus on an indigo light between your eyebrows. This is your third eye chakra, the Ajna. With every deep breath, imagine this light sharpening your inner vision, helping you see things clearly and guiding your decisions."

The indigo light felt like a bright star between my eyes, making everything seem more straightforward, as if I could see inside my thoughts.

"Lastly, picture a glowing purple light at the top of your head. This is your crown chakra, the Sahasrara. Breathe into this space, and connect yourself to the universe like you're part of everything."

I felt the purple light above my head like a crown, and I imagined myself connected to the stars, the moon, and the whole world.

"Take a deep breath, and let these lights flow together." Exaltor's voice said.

I sat there, feeling the magic swirl inside me, all the colours and lights mixing. It was like I was one with everything around me, like I could do anything.

"I will leave you to it," said Exaltor, and his cloud face disappeared.

****

Back at the castle, locked in a metal room completely bare save for a separated-by-metal-walls-and-a-door corner for sleeping. Loose ropes were scattered on the floor next to the hostages, looking all tangled up.

Exaltor, who was trying to stay calm, looked around at everyone. His voice was both profound and comforting. "Do nothing," he told them quietly, "even if Polliexa taunts you and you feel like fighting back. Help is on the way, but you must stay calm. It'll all be ruined if we do anything that makes her suspicious."

They all nodded, trying our best to keep still. It was hard, though, especially with all the bad things Polliexa could say and do. But Exaltor was right—if they wanted a chance to escape, they had to trust that help was coming. So, they just waited, doing their best not to give Polliexa a reason to get even angrier.

Out of nowhere, tentacles shot out and grabbed them! They couldn't escape! The slimy, wriggly things wrapped around them and held them so tight it felt like they couldn't breathe. Before they could even fight back, one of the tentacles shoved something cold and icky into their mouths. It was some kind of potion—gross! They could taste it slide down our throats, and instantly, they felt… weak.

It wasn't just that their bodies felt heavy and tired, but their brains were all foggy, too. It was like trying to think through a big cloud of cotton. The bad part was that they couldn't even protest. The potion was making them so weak, both in their bodies and minds, that all they could do was slump there, helpless.

And the worst part? It wasn't going to stop anytime soon.

****

Outside the Eyeball Tunnel, the soft grass was covered with the aftermath of Polliexa's big earthquake. People were lying on the ground everywhere you looked, totally out of it—like they were in a deep sleep they couldn't wake up from.

Smoky was pacing back and forth, looking grave and lost in his thoughts. He didn't even notice that everyone awake was listening to him mumble to himself. "We could use the flying spell to carry them all... but only Annie and Jack can use it! And we've gotta think about the weather, too... What if it gets awful? Should we let them rest here?"

Everyone, still dazed, shouted in one big, tired voice, "Yes!"

It was enough to snap Smoky out of his thinking. He blinked and looked around, realizing that the whole group had heard everything he said.

Smoky and his family worked together, their hands moving like magic, to summon blankets out of thin air. With Lisa and Wiseman's help, they gently laid the unconscious people down on the soft, freshly appeared blankets, making sure everyone was comfortable.

At the same time, Lisa was busy tending to Jack and Annie. She carefully changed their bandages, adding a unique and powerful medicine to help them heal, being extremely careful not to damage their wings. The other medication hadn't been working, and the poor twins were still out cold, their wounds refusing to heal.

Then, Smoky's mom, looking worried, asked, "My dear, your friends with wings must be starving. How are we going to feed them if they're still unconscious?"

Lisa overheard and walked over to them, her voice calm and reassuring. "There's a special herb on our island," she explained. "It's a blossom with iridescent pollen, pink petals, a purple stem, and thorny roots. It can feed the unconscious faster and bring them out of their deep sleep. Smoky, you'll need to find seven herb plants with attached roots. If you leave now, you might make it back in time."

Smoky's eyes widened, and he nodded. He had to hurry—Jack and Annie needed him!

Smoky frowned and asked, "Why can't I just summon the herbs here? Why do I have to go all the way to find them?"

Lisa shook her head, her face serious. "If you use magic on them, they won't work. The herbs must be picked by hand to keep their magic powers intact."

Smoky sighed but didn't waste another second. He flapped his enormous wings and shot into the sky. "I'll be back soon!" he called, zooming off.

Lisa waved after him, but she suddenly froze, remembering something important. "Wait, Smoky, wait! I have something important to tell you!"

But it was too late. Smoky was already so far ahead that he was out of sight when Lisa's words left her mouth.

# 16.
# RIDDLE OF THE SOUL AND WATER WHISPERS

Exaltor walked over to Jack and Annie, who were finally done with their chakra meditation and looking all recharged. He had a severe look on his face as he asked, "How are you both feeling? Are you ready for training? We don't have much time left if we're going to level up to beat the witch."

Jack and Annie glanced at each other, took a deep breath, and nodded, both looking nervous yet excited.

"Alright then," Exaltor said, stretching his hands, "grab on, and I'll take you to the training spot."

The twins grabbed one of Exaltor's hands, and with a significant whoosh, they were suddenly standing by a river. The place was magical: the water sparkled like diamonds, and the soft sound of it flowing was calming, like a lullaby. Plains stretched out on both sides as far as they could see, making the whole place expansive and peaceful.

Exaltor turned to them with a little grin. "Okay, first up, you're going to practice… hydromancy."

Jack and Annie looked at each other, totally puzzled. "Uh… hydromancy? What even is that?" they asked, scratching their heads.

Exaltor chuckled. "It's the art of controlling water! You can position it however you like. We're starting simple, though, and then we'll work up to the hard stuff."

He pointed to the river. "Your first task is to lift some water right off the surface. Focus, and use your magic to make drops float into the air."

Annie and Jack nodded, looking super serious. They took their spots on the riverbank, squinting at the water like it held all the world's secrets. After a few minutes of deep focus—and some funny hand-waving—the water finally listened! Little droplets lifted right off the river, hovering mid-air like a sparkly rain caught in a freeze-frame.

Exaltor gave a proud nod. "Not bad! You can stop now."

The twins grinned at each other, practically bursting with excitement. They'd done it!

"Alright, that was just a warm-up," Exaltor continued. "Now for something trickier. Your next task? Make a water walkway across the river from one bank to the other. It'll take more focus and energy, so get ready."

Jack and Annie nodded, their faces set in determined expressions. They shut their eyes tight, focusing all their energy on the river. For what felt like forever, nothing happened. But they kept going, staying laser-focused on the water. Then, out of nowhere, the water began to rise! They slowly pulled the water from one bank and stretched it to the other, forming a wobbly, shiny bridge over the river.

Once they realized they'd done it, their eyes lit up excitedly. They took their first steps onto the bridge, feeling like they were walking on air. When they finally reached the other side, Exaltor greeted them with a big smile. "You two are doing fantastic! It's time for the final task—and this one's the hardest of them all, but I know you can do it!"

He continued, "This time, I want you to generate water droplets from the air around you and shape them into anything you wish. It'll take loads of focus and energy, but I believe in you. Good luck, you two!"

Annie and Jack grinned back. "We're ready! We'll give it our best."

They stood quietly, taking a deep breath before closing their eyes again, feeling the air around them. They were ready to tackle this challenge together!

They stretched out their hands, trying to pull water droplets from the air. But...all they got were soggy, wet hands! They looked at each other, shrugged, then tried again, focusing super hard. And suddenly—yes! Water droplets began to form in their hands, resembling tiny beads. They wiggled their fingers and waved their hands, making the droplets jiggle and shimmer.

Annie concentrated, held her hands steady, and slowly shaped her water into a trident. Jack scrunched up his face, focused just as hard, and formed his face into a shiny sword. When they finished, Exaltor clapped his hands. "I've trained many wizards and enchantresses over the years, but never have I seen anyone complete this challenge as quickly as you two. You're truly the first kids to do this so easily!"

Annie and Jack, beaming with pride, grabbed Exaltor's hands. With a loud whoosh, they were sucked into a tunnel of swirling light. They felt their minds go calm, like they were getting a fresh burst of energy, and when they opened their eyes again, they were standing on a plain with a pile of sticks waiting for them.

Exaltor turned to them and said, "Alright, let's start the next step of your training!"

****

At the creepy castle, Polliexa slinked into the metal room where everyone was being held. The hostages quickly got back into their tied-up positions, pretending like they hadn't just been secretly plotting. Polliexa let out a nasty, "Heh-heh-heh," her laugh echoing off the cold walls.

"So, where are all those brave 'heroes' now? So strong, so tough! The mighty saviours of the century, too weak to fight back!" she sneered, grinning. "I thought you'd be tougher...something I could use against you!" She leaned close to Exaltor, grabbing his chin and lifting his face into the light.

Exaltor's jaw clenched, and everyone saw his hands balling into fists. His face turned red with fury, veins popping out on his neck. He wanted nothing more than to slug her right there, but Polliexa smirked, "I can still sense some strength in you, grandson. I think I'll drain you first."

Exaltor, gritting his teeth, forced himself to stay calm, but his anger only bubbled up hotter as Polliexa slithered out to practice her creepy black magic. He was so mad he started bouncing up and down. But suddenly, tentacles lashed out, grabbing him tightly. One forced the horrible weakening potion down his throat. Everything spun around him; his body went limp, and he slumped back into the corner with a thud.

But even though he couldn't move, his spirit was still fighting. All the others in the room were forced to drink the same potion, weakening them.

While Polliexa was in her creepy bedroom practising black magic, she perfected some seriously evil spells to make people spill their secrets, choke, trap them, or see terrifying illusions. She even had a mannequin that she'd brought to life to "test" all these spells on, and its haunted screams echoed through the castle's dark hallways. She seemed pleased with her work, watching with a cold smirk as the poor mannequin writhed and shuddered.

Once Polliexa had practised every spell to her dark heart's content, she sent for Wanda, who was busy hunting for treasure somewhere in a faraway kingdom. When Wanda finally returned, Polliexa cackled, "Listen up, Wanda. I'm about to start a black magic ritual that'll make me invincible, and you'll benefit from it, too! But I'll need your help."

"This ritual takes seven days," she continued. "I'll be in my secret room, and no one can bother me till it's over. While I'm busy becoming all-powerful, here's your job: you go to the metal room each day and make our dear 'heroes' feel small. Humiliate them, make them accept us as their superiors, tell them they're the losers and we're the winners."

Polliexa's eyes gleamed with a wicked plan. "Then, on the seventh day, I'll emerge with even more power, and we'll either finish them and their bratty kids once and for all... or enslave them. After that, the whole planet will bow to us—and maybe, just maybe, we'll become queens of the universe!"

Wanda gave a sneaky nod, entirely on board with Polliexa's nasty plan, and slithered off to her room to brainstorm all the horrible ways she could make the "heroes" feel like nothing. Meanwhile, Polliexa was busy gathering her creepy supplies for the significant ritual. She crept around the castle, grabbing cobwebs from the dusty old basement, snagging a strange black-and-white leaf and a tiny cauldron from her Potion Plants and Equipment room, and finally, her prized crystal ball from her quarters.

Once she had everything, she went over to her colossal bookshelf, pressed a hidden button, and opened a secret doorway. Polliexa slipped into her hidden chamber, which was super simple: just a flickering campfire and a thin, eerie cushion in the middle of the room.

With her supplies ready, she carefully placed the tiny cauldron over the fire, tossed in the cobwebs and the weird leaf, and then slid her crystal ball right under the cauldron in the flames. Strangely, it didn't melt—it just glowed. Polliexa sat cross-legged on her cushion, her eyes rolling back until only the whites showed. In a deep, eerie voice, she began chanting words in a language so old and creepy that just hearing it would probably make your skin crawl.

And as she chanted, the air in the room grew colder, and the ritual began.

****

Meanwhile, Smoky zoomed through the sky, landing softly on the island. He took a deep breath and looked around, remembering what Lisa had told him: he must find a flower with iridescent pollen, pink petals, a purple stalk, and thorny roots. It sounded mysterious in a good way, so Smoky immediately started his search.

Just then, beside a sparkling lake, he spotted it! A flower with all those colours! Excited, Smoky dashed over, but as he got closer, he realized… it was just a regular old plant and the rainbow effect: His eyes were tricked by the sunlight's reflection off the water. Disappointed, he kept looking, glancing around every corner.

Suddenly, he saw it again! This time, it was near a prickly bush. Smoky hurried over, feeling his heart thumping… only to find out it was another trick of the light!

But then… There it was again! And this time, he wasn't imagining it! A whole field of flowers stood before him, surrounded by a fence with a little gate. Smoky shaded his eyes from the sunlight to double-check, and yes! This was it—the real deal! He rushed to the gate, ready to grab the flowers, when the gate zapped him! Smoky jumped back, shaking his torched fingers in surprise. That gate was no joke!

Smoky's hands were burning, so he frantically looked around for something to extinguish the flames before he turned to toast. Then he remembered the lake! Without wasting a second, he sprinted over and jumped straight in! Ahhh, the cool water washed over his hands, and it was pure bliss. "Phew," he thought, "that was close!"

But then he remembered why he was here in the first place—those special herbs for Lisa! He jumped out of the lake, shook himself off, and raced back toward the gate.

Just as he reached it, a woman appeared out of nowhere! She had long white hair and wore nothing but a simple white gown, and she smiled at Smoky like she'd been waiting for him. "To enter," she said softly, "you must answer my riddle. I am the spirit of one of the plants in this field, and my sisters are the spirits of the other plants."

Smoky gulped. A riddle?! He'd barely escaped being fried, and now he had to solve a riddle? But he straightened up, determined to try.

The woman's eyes sparkled as she continued, "If you answer my riddle, you will set me and my sisters free, the gate will open, and the herbs will be ready for you to pick, O water-dragon Smoky." Then she gave him the riddle: "I am born when light is there, yet too much light will kill me. What am I?"

She added, "It's a tricky riddle, so here are three clues: the answer starts with an 'S', it always lies on a surface, and it has six letters. You only get one chance, so think carefully, but remember, your friends need this herb fast!"

Smoky stared at her, thinking hard. "Hmm… it starts with an S, always on a surface, and six letters." He muttered to himself, "Sea? Nah, it's too short. Sandwich? Nope, too long." Then it hit him—shadow! That fits all the clues perfectly.

With a confident grin, Smoky looked up and said, "I think the answer is… shadow!"

Smoky took a deep breath and gulped, his heart pounding as he waited for the woman to reply. She stood still momentarily, her white gown fluttering, then smiled. "Your answer is… correct! Congratulations! Thank you. For now, my sisters and I are… free!"

With those words, the woman transformed into a dazzling beam of white light that shot up into the sky. Smoky watched in awe as more beams followed her, and he guessed they were her sisters, freed at last. He quickly yanked open the gate and rushed into the field of herbs. He carefully picked seven plants, counted them, and then flew back to the campsite.

When he arrived, he zoomed through the air in a ball of shimmering scales, sliding the herbs toward Lisa. But just as he did, his feet slipped, and he tumbled onto the soft grass with a loud thud. Oof!

He blinked, disoriented, but saw the tribals kneeling in a circle, praying for Annie and Jack's safety and recovery. Smoky quickly stood up, feeling embarrassed, but watched as Lisa worked. She took the herbs he had gathered and mashed them together into a green paste. With quick hands, she fed Jack and Annie a spoonful of it, praying it would help them heal.

The tension in Smoky's chest eased as he watched his friends, hoping the magic of the herbs would work.

# 17.
# FIRE AND FORTITUDE

In the Celestium, Exaltor snapped his fingers, and — poof! — A campfire burst to life on the pile of sticks in front of Annie and Jack. He grinned and said, "Alright, it's time to learn pyromancy!"

Annie scrunched her eyebrows. "Uh... what does that mean?"

Exaltor chuckled. "It's like hydromancy, but you're controlling fire instead of water. You'll start with fire dancing. All you have to do is make the flames lean in any direction you want. Ready?"

The twins nodded, their eyes wide with excitement. They both focused on the crackling flames, watching the orange and red swirls twist around as smoke drifted up in curly spirals. Annie reached down to pull up her stocking, and the fire leaned right along with her hand just then! Her eyes went wide. She tried again, moving her hand to the side, and the fire followed, as if they were copying her. "Whoa, Jack! Look at this!"

Jack tried it, too, waving his hand in the air. Sure enough, the flames on his side bent in that direction like they were listening. Soon, the twins pulled half the fire in opposite directions, making the flames dance back and forth like two snakes in a duel.

Exaltor was happy with both of them. "Nicely done! You're both natural. Now for the next challenge…" His smile got a bit mischievous. "This time, you're going to make the campfire itself hover in the air. This one might take a bit more concentration!"

Annie and Jack exchanged an excited glance, ready to give it their best shot.

Annie and Jack took a deep breath, then stared hard at the campfire. Over and over in their minds, they chanted, *Firehoverintheair, Firehoverintheair,* until the words became a single blur. Suddenly, Annie raised her hands — and the flames lifted off the pile of sticks, floating right above her palms like she was holding a fiery balloon!

Exaltor grinned, "Nice work, Annie! Now, put the fire back on the sticks and let Jack try."

Annie carefully set the flames back down, and Jack stepped up. He focused, squeezed his eyes shut, and lifted his hands, and there it was — the fire floated up again! Exaltor's eyes sparkled. "Fantastic! You're both getting the hang of this faster than I expected! Here's your next challenge: snap your fingers and create fire from your hands, then shape that fire into any creature you like. Good luck!"

The twins nodded, glancing at each other, and then they snapped their fingers repeatedly, trying to get a spark. Nothing... but they kept snapping. Then, out of nowhere, sparks popped from both their hands, floating up and bursting into flames! With huge grins, Annie and Jack started moving their hands, pulling and shaping the fire just like they did with water.

When they were done, Annie's fire turned into a fierce lion with green, glowing eyes that looked mysterious and wild. Jack's was a fiery red eagle, with eyes a warm brown that seemed to smile. Annie made her fire-lion race back and forth, and it even roared little flames! Jack made his fire-eagle swoop through the air, looping around until it wrote JACK in the smoke!

They laughed and watched their creatures dance until Exaltor waved his hands and poof! The fire lion and fire eagle disappeared in a flash. He beamed, "Incredible work! You both nailed it! Take my hands, and let's go to the next part of your training."

Annie and Jack grabbed Exaltor's hands, hearts thumping with excitement, and in a flash — whoosh! — They were whisked away to the top of a tall, breezy hill. The wind tickled their faces, and beside them were two piles of crunchy leaves, rustling as the breeze danced around them.

Exaltor turned to them and said, "Now, you're going to practice aeromancy."

Jack's eyes lit up. "Aeromancy? Wait... is that like... magic with air?"

Exaltor nodded with a small smile. "Exactly. Aeromancy is the art of controlling and using air."

Annie and Jack looked at each other with huge grins. Exaltor pointed at the leaf piles and said, "Alright, for your first task, you each need to control the wind and blow away one pile of leaves."

****

Back at the castle, the hostages woke up groggy and nervous. They scrambled into their "position" as fast as they could when they heard footsteps echoing down the hallway. Wanda walked in, wearing this explorer getup: a khaki suit, a hat, and a belt packed with pouches and gadgets. In her front pocket, a gold penknife sparkled, with twenty attachments! She grinned at them and sneered, "Slept well last night?"

Then she chuckled, a mean, hearty laugh. "Well, well, well, Mr Grandson of Polliexa the Great," she said, glaring at Exaltor. "Got any strength left in you, or did that potion wash it all away?" She laughed again, louder this time. "Kneel before me, all of you! Polliexa and I are your superiors!"

But they didn't kneel. Wanda's smirk turned wicked, and she pointed at them with magic, forcing them down to their knees like invisible hands were pushing them down. "Good. Now for a little fun! Ah, yes — humiliation!"

She pointed her finger, and poor Evergreen found herself suddenly wearing a ridiculous, ruffled dress. Without wanting to, she started doing a silly dance, flopping around like a puppet on strings. Wanda spun around, laughing, and everyone else was dressed up goofy, too, forced into these crazy, funny dances they couldn't control. Soon, they all looked like a ridiculous lineup of silly-dancing hostages in silly clothes.

Wanda clapped her hands and squealed like a spoiled brat, "Brilliant! More! I want more humiliation!" Then she pointed her thumb at Exaltor, and, to his horror, he started dancing ballet — and his giant boots weren't helping. He tripped all over himself, looking like the world's clumsiest dancer. Meanwhile, Wonder and the fairies were made to breakdance in their pointy shoes, slipping and tumbling over each other. Wanda was laughing so hard she had tears streaming down her face, nearly splashing into the bucket of savoury mince and gummies she had conjured up to snack on while watching them dance.

Finally, when the dancing stopped, Wanda clapped like she was at some show. "Magnifico! Splendifico! Terrifico!" she cheered, mocking them. "Time for your prize! TENTACLES!"

With another clap, tentacles appeared out of nowhere, each holding a spoonful of weakening potion. Breeze whispered nervously, "But I thought only Polliexa could summon the tentacles…"

Wanda's eyes suddenly glowed red, and her voice got all wobbly and weird. "Well, now you know someone else who can, too." The tentacles forced the potion into their mouths, and one by one, they all slumped, weak and sleepy, as they were dragged off to the sleeping corner.

****

The next day, as soon as the sun peeked out, Wiseman, Lisa, and Smoky rushed over to where Annie and Jack lay, hoping they'd gotten better. They leaned over them, but… nothing. Annie and Jack were still unconscious, just lying there like they were in a deep, deep sleep. But there was one good sign—their wounds were completely gone! Smoky, always the cheery one, grinned and said, "Well, hey! At least their cuts and bruises are all healed up. That's a good start!"

Saffire thought for a moment and said, "Let's get moving. We'll carry Jack and Annie on the strong pieces of cloth. And let's mark this spot with a piece of red cloth, just in case." So, they tied a piece of bright red cloth to a nearby sapling.

Then, Sefyr, Smoky, and Saffire helped everyone pack their things. They gathered their belongings, medicines, and small supplies, firmly tied the red cloth to the sapling and headed towards the spooky castle.

After a full day of walking, everyone was exhausted. As the evening light started to fade, they paused to rest. But as they looked around, Lisa's eyes widened. "Wait a minute!" she shouted, pointing. "I see the sapling! The one with the red cloth! We're back where we started!"

Everyone gathered around the sapling, staring at it with expressions of confusion. They were wiped from all that hiking, so Wiseman finally sighed and said, "I don't know what is happening here. But whatever it is, we'll figure it out tomorrow. Right now, we need to rest up and save our energy."

## 18.
## THE CASTLE'S HIDDEN TRAIL

The twins nodded, shutting out everything except the wild wind that ruffled their hair and whooshed past their faces. It was like the wind had a life of its own, whispering secrets to them. Annie and Jack reached up, letting the wind slip through their fingers, and then—bam!—they aimed their hands at the piles of leaves, sending them flying all over, scattering like wild confetti!

Exaltor beamed and said, "Good job, you two! Now, listen up: I will throw magical objects at you. Your mission? Use the wind to blow them away. But if you can't, dodge them. Stand back-to-back and be ready!"

Annie and Jack scrambled into position, pressing their backs together. Exaltor moved out of their sight and started counting, "Three... Two... One... Go!" Suddenly, he was hurling all sorts of magical things at them—flying potion bottles, a shrivelled-up lizard (gross!), enchanted knives, and who knows what else!

The first few things caught them off guard, and they had to duck and dodge. But soon, they figured out a trick: they ran their hands through the wind, aimed at the flying object, and then whipped them to the side, sending the stuff spinning away! Then, Exaltor sped things up, throwing things faster and faster. At first, it was chaos—they had to jump aside a bunch of times—but soon enough, they got back in sync, deflecting the magical objects with ease!

Finally, Exaltor gave them a proud smile and came to a stop. "Well done, you two! Now, for your next challenge... It's time to create a windstorm—a real hurricane!"

Annie stared at the air in front of her, deep in concentration, and without even thinking, she started swirling her fingers in tiny circles. The air around her began swirling, too, picking up dust and making a mini tornado! Jack joined in, and together, they focused so hard that the air spun faster and faster until they could feel themselves almost getting pulled right into the hurricane they'd created! But just then, Exaltor gave a quick signal, and they came to a halt. The storm fizzled out, vanishing like it was never there.

The twins plopped down for a rest, totally wiped out but proud. After a while, they felt their energy return and jumped up, ready for the next challenge.

Exaltor nodded. "You look ready to go again. Now, it's time to master the second-last element: Earth! We've practised water, fire, and wind—now we move on to geomancy, the magic of controlling earth and stone."

Annie and Jack listened carefully as Exaltor explained. "Alright, hold my hand to travel to the practice spot."

They each grabbed one of Exaltor's hands, and whoosh! They were on a vast plain scattered with small stones and pebbles everywhere. The twins looked at Exaltor, waiting for their next task.

He grinned. "Your first job: gather all these scattered stones and arrange them into a circle—but remember, no touching! Use only your power and magic. Start whenever you're ready!"

****

Wanda sat in Polliexa's secret room, leaning over a crystal ball perched on a fancy gold stand. The crystal ball had swirling fog inside, almost as if it were alive, and the stand was made of pure gold, with runes carved all over it. She was doing her usual check-up on all the traps and obstacles around the castle, but when she got to the tunnel, Smoky was… missing!

Someone had freed him. Wanda's eyes narrowed as she stared harder into the crystal ball, thinking, *Show me who freed Smoky,* and there they were—Annie and Jack, lying on pieces of cloth, looking hurt but somehow still moving.

Her face twisted with rage, and she stormed off to where her hostages were being held. Without a second thought, she flung her magic at Exaltor, slamming him against the wall! Before he could even move, she pinned him there with magic and wrapped a choking spell around his neck.

"Where are they?"

She hissed, her voice as sharp as broken glass, tightening her magic grip as Exaltor gasped for air. Wonder, and the others tried to rush to help, but Wanda just flicked her wrist, and they were thrown against the other wall, too.

Exaltor's face turned red as he rasped, "Where... are... who...?"

"Your precious kids, where are they?"

Wanda demanded, practically spitting out the words.

"I... don't... know... I... swear... I... don't... know,"

He choked out, barely able to breathe.

Wanda gave him a cruel smile. "Fine. But you'll be seeing their lifeless bodies soon enough. And if you're lying to me, I'll tear you apart piece by piece."

She let go of him with a sharp turn and swept out of the room, determined to track down Annie and Jack no matter what.

****

The next day, the tribals woke up super early, all ready to reach the castle before nightfall. They didn't want a repeat of last night's disaster, and that's when Smoky got an idea. He racked his brains and said, " I can fly towards the castle, figure out the way, and come back to guide you all!"

Everyone thought this was an excellent idea. So off Smoky flew, zooming towards the castle.

The tribals waited...and waited...and waited. By evening, they were distraught. They saw a tiny dot in the sky just as they were getting ready to look for him. It was Smoky! But he was panting hard, and suddenly he dropped right out of the sky and landed on his feet in front of them.

"I... I don't get it!" Smoky panted. "I was flying straight towards the castle the whole time. But somehow, I ended up right back here! I think we're going in circles. There's some powerful magic at work here."

The tribals all exchanged nervous looks. This wasn't just a maze. It was like the land itself was playing tricks on them.

# 19.
# WHISPERS OF THE EARTH

Annie and Jack looked at each other, their eyes asking, "You ready for this?" They both nodded quickly, then raised their hands to start the task. Annie went first, sweeping her hands from outside to inside, and she noticed a few pebbles beginning to move! She focused harder, making her hands flow like gentle waves in a river. The pebbles followed her, rolling over and forming a neat little semicircle. She took a break and let Jack have a turn. Jack copied Annie's moves and soon formed the other half of the circle.

Exaltor grinned and said, "Wow! You nailed it on the first try! Let's make it a bit tougher: lift this circle of stones and maintain its shape while it's in the air."

Annie tried first, focusing hard on the ring of stones. She squinted and put all her energy into it, but nothing happened at first. She tried again and lifted the whole thing! She even tossed it like a pizza in the air and caught it, laughing as she set it back down for Jack. Jack gave it a go, focused with all his might, and managed to lift the circle, too, putting it down carefully with a grin.

Exaltor seemed satisfied and said, "Incredible! Here's the final task: make a rock by sticking pebbles together, roll it along the path, and keep adding more pebbles to it like a magnet."

Annie and Jack got to work, gathering pebbles and sticking them together until they each had a good-sized rock. They rolled their rocks along, and with each roll, more pebbles joined. Before long, both had huge boulders as giant as they were!

Exaltor nodded, clearly impressed. "Amazing work! But be warned, my kids, Polliexa is more powerful than any of these tasks. Now, let's take it up a notch. Hold my hands; I'll bring you to the final part of your training."

Annie and Jack grabbed Exaltor's hands tightly. With a whoosh, they were suddenly standing in a beautiful field bursting with iridescent flowers! The flowers swayed in the breeze, and the warm summer sun shone, making everything feel bright and magical. Exaltor smiled like the sun and said, "Welcome to your next challenge. This is where you'll practice phytomancy."

Jack blinked, looking confused. "Phytomancy? Is that... fight, oh Nancy?"

Exaltor and Annie burst out laughing, and the sound of Annie's laugh was so loud it almost echoed. "Ha-ha-ha-ha-ha-ha-ha!

Exaltor chuckled and said, "Ha-ha-ha! No, no! It's not fight, oh Nancy! Phytomancy—P-H-Y-T-O-M-A-N-C-Y—is the art of controlling and manipulating plants. It's the hardest skill and will take all the magic and focus you've learned. Are you ready for your first task?"

Annie and Jack nodded eagerly.

"Good!" Exaltor continued, "Your first task is to make a seed grow!"

Annie and Jack looked around, excited and a little nervous. This was going to be the most complex challenge yet!

****

After Wanda stormed out of the room, Wonder rushed to Exaltor, who was gasping and unable to speak correctly without hurting his throat. She gently laid his head on her lap and whispered, "She's awful. She choked you to get information about Annie and Jack. What do they want with our kids?"

Exaltor's finger flickered weakly, and with a soft glow, he used his magic to send a few glitchy words into the air: WE NEED TO GIVE

OUR KIDS A LITTLE TIME TO ENHANCE THEIR POWERS. THEY WILL BE HERE SOON TO DEFEAT THESE WITCHES.

Wonder nodded, her face full of hope. "I know, honey. Our kids are special, and I believe in them. They're going to be fine." She smiled softly as she stroked his hair. "I hope your throat feels better by morning. For now, try to rest. You've been through enough."

Exaltor closed his eyes, comforted by her words, and finally let himself drift into a much-needed sleep.

****

Wiseman scratched his chin, thinking hard. Then, a lightbulb went off in his head. "I have an idea! This will prove if we're walking in circles for sure." He quickly explained, "We'll wish for a never-ending ball of thick wool. Two of us will roll the ball toward the castle while Smoky holds onto the other end. If they reach the castle, one will hold the ball while the other dashes back to us using super speed. If they can return to us, then Smoky's theory is true—we're somehow walking in circles."

The idea made sense to everyone, so they quickly implemented it. They chose two tribals for the task, one with superspeed. With the never-ending ball of wool in hand, the two set off, and Smoky held onto the end of the wool, watching them disappear over the horizon.

That night, as everyone settled down to sleep, they anxiously waited. Soon, the two tribals returned. Their faces were weary but determined. Everyone sat up, excited to hear their report.

"Well?" Wiseman asked, holding his breath.

The two tribals looked around, unsure, then spoke in unison, "We were walking toward the castle the whole time, but we don't know how we ended up back here. Smoky was right. We've been walking in circles."

A heavy silence fell over the group as the reality of the situation sank in. Something magical seemed to be at play, keeping them trapped in an endless loop.

# 20. WANDERLUST OF THE MIND

Exaltor snapped his fingers, and poof! A tiny seed appeared in each of Annie and Jack's hands. The seeds floated up, twirling like little magic marbles, then dropped straight into the ground. Annie and Jack crouched down, eyes glued to the spot, focusing as hard as they could to make the seeds sprout. And suddenly, little white shoots poked out of the ground! Annie and Jack doubled down on their concentration, basically willing the plants to grow faster. The sprouts stretched taller and taller until they'd grown into full trees! Annie and Jack were totally drained, so they flopped to the ground, catching their breath.

Exaltor noticed this and said, "Nice work! You've passed this challenge, though not perfectly. But don't worry; most wizards struggle with phytomancy, so it's normal. Hopefully, we won't need to use this skill much in the battle. Now, your next task is to use your tree's vines to trap your twin. If you get caught, your job is to free yourself by controlling the vines."

Annie went first. She waved her hand like she was stirring a giant pot, and the vines from her tree stretched out, wrapping all around Jack like a big green cocoon. Only his face and fingers were left poking out! Jack wiggled his fingers, channelling his magic right through them, and made the vines peel back off him and retreat up Annie's tree.

Now, it was Jack's turn. He climbed his tree, then leapt down, pulling vines along with him like they were on magic strings. He wrapped them around Annie until only her face and fingers were visible. Annie concentrated hard, her magic sparking through her fingertips, and—whoosh! The vines slipped off her and zoomed back up Jack's tree.

After that, they plopped back down, tired but proud, while Exaltor said, "You've done well. Your third and final task is to use your trees' roots to send messages to each other. All you have to do is yell your message into the roots and tell it where to go."

Exaltor snapped his fingers, and just like that, the trees slid apart until they were way across the field from each other. Annie stood by her tree, and Jack stood by his. Annie bent down to the roots, took a deep breath, and yelled, "Destination: tree at the other side of the field. Message: Jack, can you hear me?!"

Exaltor nodded and said, "Now, snap your fingers to make the message travel to Jack."

Annie snapped her fingers as loud as she could—so loud that her whole hand tingled. Instantly, she felt a weird, high-pitched squealing in her ears as her message zoomed across the field to Jack. Over at his tree, Jack heard it and grinned. He yelled into his tree root, "Destination: tree at the other side of the field. Message: Yep, Annie! Loud and clear!"

Just then, like magic, Exaltor appeared beside Jack and said, "The message is ready. Now, snap your fingers to send it to Annie."

Jack snapped his fingers super hard—so hard that a tiny flame sparked on his hand! He quickly put his fingers in his mouth to put it out just as the high-pitched squeal zoomed back across to Annie's tree.

Exaltor watched them proudly and said, "You two did better than I expected. Rest up because we'll be off to the final training spot when you're ready."

They did as Exaltor said, shutting their eyes tight and getting ready for the last challenge. Suddenly, they felt like they were flying, and when they opened their eyes, they were in this massive grassland that seemed to stretch on forever. Nothing but endless green grass swaying in the wind all around them!

Exaltor's voice boomed, "I will return your spirits to your real bodies after this one final challenge—you're almost at the witch's castle!"

Annie and Jack glanced at each other, excitement and a little bit of fear in their eyes. This was the last big test before they'd be face-to-face with the witch herself!

****

The prisoners in the castle scrambled into their usual spots when they saw Wanda stomping back in, looking as grumpy as a storm cloud from last night. She snapped, "Let's play Chinese Whispers today! And if the last person gets it wrong, I'll give you all a sip of your favourite... weakening potion!"

Everyone exchanged wide-eyed looks like, *Huh?! Chinese Whispers? She usually treated us like dust on her heels!*

Wanda leaned close to Exaltor's ear and whispered, "Better butter." But Exaltor just froze. Wanda leaned closer and hissed, "Pass it on, or someone's getting slapped to sleep."

Gulping, Exaltor quickly whispered to Wonder, who whispered to Pleasant, who whispered it down the line to all the fairies until it reached the last fairy, Spirit. Wanda clapped her hands and asked Spirit, "So, what did you hear my little whisper fairy?"

Spirit took a deep breath, "Better butter!"

Wanda's face lit up in fake excitement. "Oh, my goodness! Genie macaroni! You're right! It is better butter!" Everyone cheered for Spirit, relieved they wouldn't have to drink that nasty potion. But then Wanda sneered, "Guess what? You all get a prize! Tentacles!"

Before anyone could blink, slimy tentacles appeared, grabbing everyone and forcing that awful potion down their throats. They spluttered, "But you said we wouldn't have to drink it if we got it right!"

Wanda laughed, her voice echoing like a wicked spell, "You thought I wouldn't give you the potion just because you got one silly answer right? Oh, you poor, foolish creatures! Aha-ha-ha-ha-ha-ha-ha-ha-ha-ha!"

And as her cackle faded, everyone's limp bodies were dragged back to the sleeping corner, groaning and dazed.

****

Out in the field, the tribals were racking their brains, trying to figure out how to reach the castle without going in circles. Suddenly, Lisa piped up, "Let's not give up yet. Let's try one more time!"

So off they went again, straggling through the night. But when they stopped for a break, they looked around—and for the seventh time, they were back at the same spot! By now, everyone's spirits were as low as a slug's. They plopped down, sighing and bemoaning, starting to wonder what would happen if they never reached the castle.

Wiseman wandered to one of the empty tents, crossed his legs, and closed his eyes. He thought we'd been trying to find answers outside this whole time. Maybe I need to look inside myself.

He dived deep into his thoughts, searching every corner of his mind for a way out of their circle-trap. And then—he had a vision! There was a flyphant in his mind—a flying elephant with pure white wings! It flapped its wings and spoke: "Don't be afraid; I am your inner voice. The field you're in is like a mirror. When you walk forward, you're going backwards. To reach your goal, you must walk backwards, keeping the castle in sight. If you do this, the castle will come closer and closer until you're right there!"

Wiseman's eyes snapped open. He jumped up and called everyone over. They all listened as he explained the vision. The idea seemed wild, but they were desperate enough to try it!

They packed up, took down the tents, and with Wiseman leading, they all started walking backwards, keeping their eyes on the castle.

Slowly, step by step, the castle got bigger and bigger until—finally!—they stopped and found themselves just a short distance from the castle gates.

They wanted to jump and shout for joy, but they celebrated quietly in case the witch, Polliexa, was listening in.

# 21.
# A HARBINGER OF DREAD

Exaltor looked at Annie and Jack with his grave, wise face and said, "Alright, for your last challenge, I need to see if you can handle wind, lightning, and earth all at once. Polliexa is as wild and powerful as a thunderstorm. If you can master a thunderstorm, you'll have a chance against her. So, here's what you must do: crack open the ground beneath you using lightning and hide the storm inside it. If you can't, pull water out of thin air and throw it onto the storm to put it out."

Then Exaltor stared hard at the air in front of him, and a spark of lightning shot right into the ground, and a thunderstorm flared to life in front of them, crackling and rumbling. Annie and Jack zoomed up to the storm, their deep hole in the ground ready to trap it. But right then, they spotted two figures in the storm's eye. They squinted through the chaos, and their great-grandparents were floating in the centre, reaching out to them!

Annie and Jack flew closer, right into the eye of the storm. Just then, the clouds split open, and a bright white light streamed from their great-grandparents' hands, hitting Annie and Jack right in their chests. The lightning from the storm merged with the light, filling their bodies with a crackling, buzzing power. Then, just as suddenly as they had appeared, their great-grandparents faded away.

Annie and Jack floated back down on the now-pure-white thunderclouds, landing softly on the ground. Exaltor stared at them, blinking in amazement. "Well, that was… completely unexpected," he said, shaking his head slowly. "Looks like you've gained an extra power—the power to control lightning."

Exaltor looked super serious as he said, "Alright, it's time to get your spirits back into your bodies since you're getting close to the witch's castle now. You've got to be ready to fight because she's started stealing our powers."

Then, Exaltor and the whole field started flickering like a video game glitch. "She's already taking my power—that's why I'm glitching!" he said, sounding weird and echoey. "By the time the moon goes all dark at midnight tonight, she'll have sucked up all our powers. And after that… she's going to destroy our village!"

Annie and Jack looked at each other with wide eyes, feeling the weight of what was coming. This was it—the showdown with the witch!

****

As Annie and Jack woke up, the air felt like it was buzzing. They could hear voices—Lisa, Wiseman, and Smoky—talking beside them. Smoky sounded super worried, as if he was about to explode with questions.

"Lisa, Smoky's right," came a voice filled with urgency. "Do you know when the twins will finally wake up?"

"They're close. I can feel it. They're waking up today," Lisa replied, her voice confident.

And just like that, Annie's eyes popped open with a whoosh. She first saw a huge, creepy, pitch-black castle before them. Lisa, Wiseman, and Smoky noticed her waking up, too, staring at her in shocked silence. Annie shot up, her wings snapping open, and joined Jack at the front to check out the castle.

The carvings on the castle walls looked like giant, broken hearts, with a huge "W" in the middle that made them look like they had been split in half, and a creepy "P" carved into the top of the broken hearts. Just as they were taking it all in, the whole army skidded to a stop.

The whole army instantly poured out of the camp, buzzing with whispers. Everyone looked worried, asking, "Are they okay?" and "What happened to them?" as they stared up at the ginormous fortress in awe.

Jack and Annie quickly told Smoky about all their training to fight Polliexa and spilled out their brave plan. Wiseman explained that before they could save their parents and everyone else locked up there, they'd have to defeat two scary beasts Polliexa kept inside the castle.

They wasted no time. The army split up: one group got ready to battle the first beast, and the other was set to back up Jack and Annie with the second one. Together, they marched toward the castle with a fierce, determined look in their eyes.

When Annie knocked hard on the massive door, it creaked open, echoing through the dark halls. Torches flickered to life as the army stepped forward, disappearing into the castle's shadowy depths.

The flickering torchlight threw weird shadows as they faced their first enemy: a terrifying creature covered in stinky goat's blood and slimy goo—a chupacabra! Ready to give battle, Jack and Annie were held back by Wiseman, who imparted vital knowledge on defeating the beast. He rallied the army firmly, invoking their courage and determination to stand against the looming threats. "Fight wisely, and may God's blessings be with you," Wiseman encouraged, his words resonating with unwavering faith. The army's resounding cry, "We fight, Wiseman!" echoed through the air, a testament to their shared determination.

As they pressed onward, they encountered the second beast, a nightmarish blood demon cloaked in darkness. They engaged the creature with grim determination, plunging into a perilous battle within the spiralling staircase leading to Polliexa's lair.

Meanwhile, deep in Polliexa's hidden room, she cast a spell to drag Exaltor, Wonder, and the fairies into a trap. They were wrapped tight in sticky spider silk, and the window was angled just right to catch the lunar eclipse. Polliexa didn't even blink, still focused on her creepy ritual. Wanda stood by her side, ready to jump in if anything went wrong.

But just as Polliexa's eyes were about to glow and start stealing their powers, something unexpected happened. Her eyes snapped wide open! She gasped, realizing the secret room was in the wrong spot for the lunar eclipse. "We'll finish this in my quarters!" she hissed. "Let's go!"

With a flick of her hand, Polliexa and Wanda dragged the hostages down the winding hallway just in time for the moon to rise. As soon as they reached Polliexa's quarters, the final phase of the ritual began—but then, the door flew open, and there stood Annie and Jack, ready to stop her!

# 22.
# A GAME OF DECEIT

The room was enormous, like one of those grand ballrooms in a castle. In two corners were these super cool four-poster beds with curtains, and between them was a big, creepy window that looked out into the night. In another corner were squishy, comfy chairs and ottomans, where Polliexa probably liked to sit and read her peculiar, dark books.

But the fourth corner? That's where things got spooky. This humongous cauldron was so big it took up almost a quarter of the room! Polliexa probably used it to make her gross, bubbly potions. Next to the cauldron were two massive desks. One was Polliexa's, piled high with scrolls and weird tools for her evil experiments. Beside it was a cupboard stuffed with her matching black gowns and creepy cosmetics. Wanda's desk and cupboard were right next to Polliexa's, filled with the same kind of spooky stuff for herself. It was like an evil scientist's lair mixed with a fancy dressing room!

Polliexa was with her BFF, Wanda, soaking up power like greedy magic sponges. Meanwhile, their poor hostages were slumped against Polliexa's huge, creepy bed, their energy draining away and zapping straight into Polliexa and Wanda. Wanda still had her little pocket knife.

Polliexa paused her magic and sneered, "I knew you'd come here to save your parents. How adorable, thinking you're the heroes when you're the ones who need rescuing. Oh, a child's sweet, foolish love for its parents." She cackled like she'd just won an evil villain award.

Before Jack and Annie could say a word, they were wrapped up tight in sticky spider silk, their mouths gagged so they couldn't even shout. Their torches clattered to the ground, one still flickering with a brave little flame. The flame rolled closer until it stopped at Exaltor's feet.

He glanced down, scooped up the fire in his hands like it was no big deal, and started melting the silk binding him. Annie noticed him out of the corner of her eye, her heart pounding. Exaltor caught her look and gave her a tiny nod: Don't blow it! Just keep staring at Polliexa.

Annie obeyed, keeping her gaze locked on Polliexa's smug face, while Exaltor moved quickly, burning through the bindings on himself and the other hostages. He gave Annie another secret nod, promising her silently: I'm coming for you and Jack next.

Annie gave Exaltor a quick, secret signal with her hands, asking to pass some of the flames to her. Exaltor nodded slightly and passed a tiny flicker of flames to Annie once he'd finished freeing the others. Like a delicate butterfly, she caught it carefully and used it to burn through the sticky spider silk binding her and Jack.

They stayed still, acting as if nothing had happened. They just sat there, pretending they were still tied up tight while Polliexa droned on and on, her voice dripping with fake pity. "You think taking away my happiness will make you the hero? Ha! It will only turn you into a villain. And, oh, sweet children, haven't you learned? Villains never win. You've always thought I was the villain, but maybe, just maybe, it's you. Still have something to say? Go on, then. I'm not so terrible that I'll take away your right to speak, even though you've taken away everything from me."

With a snap of Polliexa's fingers, the gags were sliced open, and Jack and Annie could finally talk. Jack wasted no time. He looked Polliexa straight in the eye, his voice steady and filled with truth. "Great-grandmother Polliexa, do you not see? Wanda has been using you this whole time. She tricked you and brainwashed you to use black magic, knowing it would force our great-grandfather to banish you from the village. She's always wanted our town for herself. She's not your friend, Polliexa. She's your enemy."

Jack's words hung like a storm cloud about to burst. Would Polliexa listen? Or would she consider it another "silly child's tale"? Annie and Jack held their breath, hoping she'd see the truth.

Jack's voice was steady but filled with something like hope. "Great-grandmother, our great-grandfather didn't banish you because he hated you. He did it because he saw you and Wanda as dangerous to the village. That's what leaders have to do—protect their people, no matter how hard it is. Our parents tried hard to make you see the truth, but Wanda… she twisted your mind. She made you believe we hated you, but it's not true. It's never been true! You believed her lies, and we… we've always loved you."

Polliexa's sharp, angry gaze softened just a little, her eyes flickering with something that felt like… doubt. The room seemed to hold its breath. Annie's heart leapt—was it working? Was Polliexa starting to see the truth?

It was like the light was coming back to her as if she were teetering on the edge of coming back to the good side. But then, Wanda strolled in, her heels clicking against the floor, her smirk wider than ever. She leaned in close to Polliexa, her lips curling into a sneaky grin as she whispered something right into Polliexa's ear.

Whatever it was, it made Polliexa freeze. Her face went blank, her hands clenching into fists as that flicker of hope in her eyes vanished, swallowed up by something dark.

Jack and Annie's hearts sank. Whatever Wanda had just said, it was like she'd taken the truth and crushed it into dust.

## 23.
## WAR AND LOSS: THE PRICE OF VICTORY

Wanda whipped her arm out, and a searing fire shot straight toward Annie and Jack. But instead of panicking, they stood their ground, teaming up to send the fiery blast back at her like a boomerang.

Wanda smirked and absorbed the beam like nothing, but it wasn't the same when she threw it back. Now it was spinning like a wild drill, covered in scary, spiky flames that looked like they could shred anything in their path. Jack acted fast, catching the fiery drill mid-air and transforming it into a glittering unicorn with a spear-sharp horn aimed at Wanda.

But Wanda wasn't fazed. With a flick of her hand, she turned the unicorn into a roaring chainsaw that buzzed angrily as it came flying back. Before it could reach them, Exaltor jumped in. With a wave of his hand, he reshaped the chainsaw into a handle with a spear, sword, mace, and battle axe attached, all bristling with spikes. The thing spun through the air so fast that Wanda couldn't stop it with her magic.

At the last second, Wanda flicked open a tiny mirror hidden in her pocket knife. The weapon bounced off and flew out the open window, disappearing into the night. Wanda grinned triumphantly as spider silk shot from nowhere, trapping Jack, Annie, and Exaltor again. This time, the silk smothered the flames in their hands, leaving them powerless.

But Annie wasn't done yet. With a fierce look, she summoned a roaring gust of wind inside the room. It started as a little breeze, but Jack,

Exaltor, and their loyal friend Breeze joined in, turning it into a raging, icy storm that felt like it came straight from the North Pole. The wind whipped around the room, chilling everyone except the four of them.

Polliexa stepped forward, her eyes blazing as she stretched out her hands. She looped her magic around the storm, trying to control it. She tightened her grip, pulling and straining to make it disappear. But the storm fought back, wild and untamed. Finally, with a considerable effort, Polliexa flung the storm upward. It spiralled higher and higher, crashing into the roof!

Everyone froze as the sound of breaking wood and tiles filled the room. Dust and debris rained down, and the storm ripped the entire roof off, carrying it into the sky. Polliexa turned back to them with a sly smile that practically screamed, "How's that for magic?"

Suddenly, Jack clenched his fists, and a tiny lightning bolt appeared. It was so small it looked like a sparkler at a birthday party. "Ugh, seriously?" Jack groaned, clearly disappointed.

Moonlight, always watching, smiled slyly. She deftly edged her pinkie finger out like it was a magic wand and conjured nine more lightning bolts. They zoomed toward Jack's little spark, merging into one gigantic, crackling ball of pure energy. The room lit up like fireworks as the massive ball of lightning whooshed toward Wanda, swallowing her whole and locking her inside. Her frantic spells bouncing around inside the lightning prison echoed like thunder.

Polliexa didn't waste a second. With a flick of her wrist, she pulled a shimmering potion out of thin air—like she had a secret stash of magic up her sleeve. She hurled the potion at the lightning ball, and with a loud sizzle, the ball fizzled out of existence, leaving Wanda standing there, looking frazzled.

"It's like being cooked alive in the sun!" Wanda gasped, wiping sweat off her forehead. "I'm gonna need an ice bath the size of a swimming pool!"

But Annie wasn't done yet. With a mischievous grin, she stomped her foot, and a green creeper plant shot out from under her toes. It snaked across the floor, growing bigger and faster with every second. Leaves sprouted, roots tangled, and the vine zoomed toward Wanda and Polliexa, aiming to wrap them up like a present.

Jack and Evergreen jumped in, sending their energy to supercharge the vine. It moved so fast it was like watching a time-lapse of a jungle growing in seconds. Just as the vine curled around Wanda and Polliexa's ankles, Polliexa's sharp eyes caught it.

"Not today!" she snapped. With a flick of her magic, the vine vanished into thin air, and Annie, Jack, and Evergreen suddenly found their toes stuck together like they'd been glued. Annie groaned, "Oh, come on! That was our best one yet!"

Jack and Annie wriggled their hands, even tied up, and splashed together a little puddle under Polliexa and Wanda. It wasn't much—just a splashy mess. But Ripple saw it, grinned, and made it grow. The puddle turned into a swirling, bottomless whirlpool that began sucking everything nearby.

"Uh-oh," Wanda squealed, gripping Polliexa's arm.

But Polliexa wasn't fazed. With a dramatic yank, she pulled them both free from the whirlpool's grasp, lifted the entire spinning pool into the air like it weighed nothing, and hurled it over the wall. The massive whirlpool melted away into the earth outside. Then she turned back to Jack and Annie with an intense glare that could melt ice.

Annie and Jack weren't giving up. "Okay, Plan B!" Jack whispered. They concentrated on the stones scattered across the floor, trying to make a giant boulder to crush Polliexa and Wanda. But all they got was a pile of medium-sized rocks.

"Better than nothing!" Annie shouted, and they began pelting the rocks at Polliexa and Wanda. Seeing their struggle, Pleasant grabbed a leftover rock and worked her magic. The rock continued to grow until it became a massive boulder. With a mighty heave, Pleasant sent it flying. Polliexa and Wanda toppled over like bowling pins, groaning and clutching their backs.

"You little pests!" Polliexa snarled, giving them a look that screamed, Now you've done it!

Annie suddenly had another idea, and her eyes lit up with determination. She closed her eyes, her mind buzzing with a silent chant: Let me break into Wanda's mind. Jack, Exaltor, and Spirit heard her thoughts and joined in. Their collective chant created an invisible force that shot straight into Wanda's mind.

With a loud gasp, Wanda collapsed like a puppet with its strings cut. Polliexa rushed to her side, panicked. But before she could help, Wanda's wild and defiant eyes snapped open.

Jack suddenly commanded Wanda to slap Polliexa. Wanda's hand flew up and slapped Polliexa so hard she stumbled backwards, landing near the hostages. A bright red handprint burned on Polliexa's cheek, and her shocked face was priceless.

Then, to everyone's surprise, Wanda obeyed Annie's command, shot up, and started running around the room, screaming, "I DON'T WANT TO BE EVIL! I WANT TO BE GOOD!"

Jack and Annie exchanged triumphant grins. "Guess she finally figured it out," Jack said, chuckling.

Polliexa's belly caved in as Wanda's punch landed squarely, obeying Jack. Polliexa groaned, clutching her stomach like she'd eaten a thousand rotten eggs. But, of course, being Polliexa, she wasn't down for long. With a flick of her fingers and a quick spell, the tummy ache vanished in the blink of an eye.

While everyone else was scrambling out of Wanda's mind, Wanda crumpled to the floor like a puppet whose strings had snapped. Polliexa darted to her side. "Wanda! Are you okay?"

Wanda's eyes rolled up, and for a second, she looked more like a ghost than a witch. But then, just like that, she shot upright.

"ARE YOU CRAZY?!" Polliexa shrieked. "You slapped me, punched me, and now you're acting like nothing happened?!"

Wanda blinked, looking confused. "What are you even talking about? I didn't do any of that! Why would I hit you?"

Polliexa huffed, brushing off the whole thing. "Whatever. I forgive you. Let's finish this once and for all."

With that, Polliexa and Wanda unleashed their magic at Annie and Jack, fiery bolts streaking across the room like laser beams. As determined as ever, Annie and Jack fought back with their magic. But they were just kids, and their magic wasn't strong enough to hold off the witches for long. The crackling bolts of Polliexa's and Wanda's magic edged closer and closer.

"Not today!" shouted Wonder and Exaltor as they jumped in, adding their power to the fight. All the fairies joined in one by one, their combined magic pushing back against the witches. The clash of spells created a glowing, multicoloured bubble of energy. It swirled and shimmered like an enormous soap bubble, yet trapped all its power inside, growing bigger and brighter.

Polliexa grinned wickedly, surging her magic into the bubble. Slowly, it started inching toward Annie and Jack.

Meanwhile, Smoky, fighting the terrifying chupacabra outside, scorched the beast with a blast of fire, leaving it crumpled on the ground. As the smell of smoke filled the air, Smoky spotted the blazing light coming from inside. His dragon instincts kicked in, and he flew to investigate.

Inside the room, he saw the energy bubble hovering dangerously close to his friends. Thinking fast, Smoky unleashed a stream of fire at the bubble, trying to push it back toward the witches. Instead, the bubble trembled, cracked, and began to burst.

"Get down!" Smoky roared, wrapping his massive wings around Jack, Annie, and the others.

Polliexa and Wanda made a magic shield and dived behind it, hiding like cowards. The bubble exploded with a deafening sound, flooding the room with blinding white light and a rush of energy that felt like a thousand storms had been loose.

The blast slammed into Smoky's right wing, throwing him against the wall like a rag doll. He crumpled to the floor, his wing twisted at a horrifying angle, blood dripping onto the stone. The sight of the towering dragon—his majestic wing shattered and useless—made everyone's hearts sink.

But Smoky, the braveheart, slowly stood up, his golden eyes burning with determination. Polliexa and Wanda, meanwhile, burst into laughter, their cackles echoing off the walls.

"Look at you now, you overgrown lizard!" Polliexa sneered. "You're grounded for good! Ha-ha-ha! Did you think you could beat me with these amateurs?"

Wanda joined in, her voice dripping with mockery. "You're nothing but an enslaved dragon, Smoky! Always were, always will be!"

But Smoky's eyes narrowed, his fiery gaze locking onto the witches. Despite his pain, despite their taunts, there was a storm brewing in his chest—a storm they wouldn't see coming.

Smoky leaned down and whispered something super-secret into Jack's ear. Then, in a voice that shook the room, he turned to Polliexa, his eyes blazing.

"Oh, you think this is all a big joke?" Smoky roared, his tail smashing the floor behind him. "How would you feel if I broke your arm and started laughing? First, you kidnapped me. Then you erased my memories, took away my voice, hurt me, mocked me, and still, you're not satisfied?!"

As Smoky's words echoed through the room, Jack quietly crept behind him, finger at the ready. While Polliexa and Wanda were too busy sneering at Smoky, Jack shot a sleeping spell straight at Wanda. She laughed even as it hit her, the sound getting slower and softer until she toppled to the floor with a loud thud, fast asleep.

Polliexa spun around at the noise. Her face twisted in fury, but her expression crumbled as she took in the scene—Wanda unconscious, her enemies united, and herself outnumbered nine to one. For a moment, Polliexa stood frozen, her eyes darting around the room. Then, sorrow washed over her face.

This is it, she thought. They'll finish me off. After all I've done, I deserve it.

But instead of attacking, the heroes just stood there, watching her. Their faces weren't filled with hate or anger. They looked… sorry for her.

Polliexa's lip trembled, and her voice cracked as she said, "What do you want from me now? Kill me and be done with it. Or will you humiliate me like I deserve?"

Annie stepped forward, her voice gentle but firm. "We won't kill you. Because you're the sister of the kindest sorcerer who ever lived, there's still good in you. We know it."

Polliexa's eyes welled with tears, and her hands shook. "But… I am evil," she whispered. "I've done terrible things to you all. You could strike me down right now, and no one would blame you."

Jack shook his head. "No, Polliexa. You're not evil. Wanda twisted you into thinking you were. She made you believe lies about yourself."

Before anyone could say more, Wanda's eyes snapped open. She jumped to her feet, her face contorted with fury. "You dare… You dare to put a sleeping spell on me?" she screeched. Her hands lit up with a dangerous spell aimed straight at Jack.

Polliexa gasped and leapt between them. "Stop right there!" she shouted, one hand raised to shield Jack, the other wiping the tears from her face.

Wanda's sneer grew sharper. "Oh, so now you're on their side? You spineless traitor!" she snarled. Her hand dipped into her pocket, pulling out a golden dagger that gleamed with magic. Wanda hurled it through the air with a flick of her wrist, the blade spinning toward Polliexa.

"NO!" cried Wonder as she darted forward. Grabbing Polliexa by the arm, she spun her out of harm's way, letting the dagger strike her chest instead.

Wonder gasped, her magic seeping from the wound like sparkling mist. The air around her shimmered as her power flowed toward Elsa's home in the Enchanted Lands. With the last strength, Wonder raised her hands, summoning sharp icicles that hurtled toward Wanda's heart. The icy shards struck true, blasting Wanda out the window into the night, where she vanished into the darkness.

Wonder fell to the ground, her energy gone. Polliexa caught her in her arms, her tears falling like rain. "You… you saved me?" Polliexa sobbed. "After everything I've done to you?"

Wonder smiled weakly, her voice a faint whisper. "I care about you, Polliexa… because we're family."

And with those final words, Elsa's daughter closed her eyes for the last time.